TRUE GHOST STORIES FOR KIDS

Fifty Spine-Tingling Ghostly Tales

Barbara Smith

True Ghost Stories for Kids
Fifty Spine-Tingling Ghostly Tales
Barbara Smith
ISBN: 9781980260783
@2016 Barbara Smith
Published 2016 by Barbara Smith

Table of Contents

Toy Stores R Spooky

There are lots of made-up tales about haunted toy stores but in California there's a toy store that really is haunted. The Toys R Us store in Sunnyvale, California, has a long and well-deserved reputation for being haunted.

Some people are surprised to learn about this haunting. They say that the store looks too shiny and new to be haunted. But the land on which the store was built had its own history and it is that history which has caused the store to be haunted.

The ghost's activities were well known by the time the store's employees invited a psychic, someone who's sensitive to ghosts, to come into the store and investigate. The psychic identified the spirit right away. She said that he had been a ranch-hand for the land's previous owner. His name was Johnny Johnson, but the poor soul had been known as "Crazy Johnny." He died in an accident on the farm in 1884 and it would seem that his restless spirit still haunts the property.

Although some employees in the toy store have been frightened by Johnny's ghostly antics, the psychic reported that his spirit is harmless. She called him a "forlorn soul." Even so, employees get upset when they tidy the store at night only to unlock the doors the next morning and find books lying on the floor and roller skates and toys scattered about.

During the day the ghost can make a nuisance of himself too. He taps workers on their shoulders and runs his ghostly hands through their hair. Some people even hear their names called when no one is there. Well, no one in this life, anyway.

Johnny's ghost can be quite loud. He has been known to scream, "Let me out, let me out," from inside an empty and enclosed space. His footsteps have also been heard walking around in vacant sections of the store. He's even been credited with turning on the taps in the women's washroom when no one is anywhere near them and one aisle of the store will occasionally and quite mysteriously smell of fresh flowers.

Years ago a staff member watched anxiously as stock flew off the shelves, not from customer sales but as a result of a ghostly prank. (Doesn't that make you wonder if any of those toys were Casper the Friendly Ghost dolls?)

Despite all his ghostly hijinks, the employees at Toys R Us in Sunnyvale, California enjoy having Johnny as part of their team. And that's just as well because it seems that

Johnny is determined to spend his afterlife where he lived, even if it's not a farm anymore.

Talking Terror

We've all had a favourite toy, one that we cherish beyond all others, so much so that even when we outgrow it, that toy still holds a special place in our hearts. When that treasure is a doll or a stuffed animal, the little plaything can really feel like a friend and we treat it that way, taking it with us wherever we go and, if we can't take it along, we leave our little friend in a special place, often on our bed.

That's exactly how it was for a little boy we'll call Danny, who lived with his parents on an isolated property in north-western Canada. His favourite Christmas present the year he was four was a bright red stuffed animal that talked when you squeezed the toy's hand. It's no wonder the boy was so partial to his soft, talkative new friend. You see there weren't any other kids living nearby, so the stuffie became Danny's substitute friend. He named his new friend Elmer. The two would chat together all day long, even while Danny was also playing with other toys. Of course, they couldn't have a real conversation because Elmer just had a few phrases and songs programmed into his voice box but Danny didn't seem to mind.

The only time the two were ever separated was at bedtime because Danny's mother didn't want her son disturbing himself by rolling over in his sleep and accidentally triggering Elmer's voice box. Fortunately, Danny was an obedient boy so there was never a problem. Well, not until the day the stuffed toy began talking and singing when no one was anywhere near it. Worse, Elmer's voice changed to a low hissing growl and the innocent-looking stuffie didn't just ask to be tickled; instead it made really rude comments and when it sang it certainly didn't sing a sweet little version of the alphabet song.

Danny's mother couldn't always figure out what the toy was saying but she knew the voice sounded nasty. She tried not to be scared and told herself that the sounds must have been planted by an employee at the toy factory with a warped sense of humour. But she didn't always believe herself.

By summer, Danny's mother figured she had put up with the foul-mouthed toy for quite long enough so one night, after her son was fast asleep, she sneaked into his bedroom, took a deep breath for courage and plucked Elmer from the shelf. Her hands shook as she carried the toy outside. She was half expecting it to tell her to put it down but then she told herself that was a ridiculous thought because, after all, this was just a toy.

She carried the ball of red fur outside feeling more fool-ish than frightened. After all, it looked and even felt just like an ordinary toy. Despite that, she buried the toy at the far edge of the side yard and as deep in the ground as she possibly could.

The next morning when Danny asked where Elmer was, his mother lied to him. She told him that a family had stopped by late the night before. They'd lost their way and were all feeling frightened and lonely, especially their 3-year-old daughter. She'd given the family directions to town and then she gave the little girl the talking Elmer.

"You'll be starting kindergarten in a few weeks Danny, so you'll have lots of real kids for friends. That little girl needed Elmer more than you did," she concluded hoping her shaking voice didn't give away her lie.

Danny looked sad for a minute but once he thought about going to school and all the kids he'd get to play with there. He felt so much better that he never mentioned his Elmer doll again. Nor did his mother, although she thought of the unnatural toy every time she looked at that patch of ground in the side yard. That bare patch of ground—where no grass, or flowers, or even weeds, ever grew again.

Spectral Skaters

Central Park in New York City is an almost magical place—an enormous and beautiful park right in the heart of that huge city. On winter evenings the grounds become even more enchanting as skaters enjoy gliding across a frozen pond to the tempo of waltz tunes broadcast through big outdoor speakers.

Skaters in formal dress glide effortlessly around the outside of the rink while other couples with colourful jackets and scarves hold hands and smile as though they don't have a care in the world. Boys wearing hockey skates chase each other around the rink hoping to impress the girls who are trying their very best not to look impressed. At the edge of the ice, a little girl wearing a powder blue zippered jacket and a tiny matching flared skirt pirouettes with more confidence than skill. All in all, it's a lovely winter sight.

Near the center of the rink, two young women, their arms linked, skate together with military precision as if they're drawing perfect figure eights on the ice with their skate blades. They're dressed in long woollen coats cinched at the waist. These girls are Janet and Rosetta Van Der Voort, sisters whose home is a brownstone mansion on 14th Street near Fifth Avenue, not far from Central Park.

Both Janet and Rosetta love to skate and they spend hours and hours perfecting their skills. Local rumour has it that their father is so strict with his daughters that he won't let them out of the house by themselves, except to go skating. If you watch the two of them for just a little while, you might notice something extraordinary: the Van Der Voort girls' skates don't quite touch the ice but float, just slightly above the frozen surface. That's because the sisters are ghosts. They died long ago, within months of each other, way back in 1880.

Every year though, people still report seeing the ghostly sisters enjoying in their afterlife, the only freedom they were allowed during their earthly lives.

Little Girl in White

There is an interesting fragment of a ghostly tale from Canada's east coast, in the province of New Brunswick. It seems that folks who have come to a particular intersection of two country roads, have been startled by what they've seen there—a beautiful little girl. They say that she appears suddenly and seemingly out of nowhere wearing an old-fashioned white dress with white shoes and socks. Her blond hair hangs in ringlets.

Anyone who has ever seen the little image is troubled because the child's shoulders are slumped and her head is down as though she's terribly unhappy. If someone approaches her to offer help, the apparition dissolves into a mist of tiny sparkles and then vanishes.

The child's identity remains a mystery. All that is known for certain is that the sight of her saddened soul has not changed a bit even though her spirit has haunted the crossroads for more than a hundred years.

As with many tales from the world of ghosts, a world

that escapes our complete understanding, we can only wonder about who she was when she was alive and why her image has remained to haunt the particular place that it has.

Boogey Nights

THUNK!

"What was that?" Jeremy exclaimed angrily as his truck crawled to a halt.

He slammed his hand on the steering wheel and jumped out of the truck. Even in his anger and frustration, he remembered to lift the truck's rusty old hood carefully. The catch didn't have very many more openings or closings left in it. Jeremy certainly didn't need to have that break too, on top of whatever else had broken down.

Peering under the truck's hood, Jeremy saw that the fan belt had completely torn apart. He looked up at the sky. It was getting dark. He hadn't planned on making this trip in the first place but this was an emergency. His father had been taken to the hospital and Jeremy very much wanted to be there for him.

Sure hope someone's home at that house I just passed, he thought as he grimly trudged back along the dusty road and up to the small, weather-beaten house he had just driven by.

Lights were shining in the windows and there was music coming from within. Jeremy smiled with relief. If he could get a replacement part for his truck he could get back on the road again before nightfall. Then maybe this trip wouldn't take as long as he'd feared.

As he approached the little house, Jeremy realized that the front door didn't look as though it had ever been used, so he followed the gravel driveway around to the back door. He knocked quietly at first, not wanting to startle whoever was inside. As he waited for the door to open, Jeremy realized that the music he'd heard wasn't from a radio or a stereo. It was live music. *Musicians must be practicing inside!* Jeremy thought and knocked again, louder this time.

Seconds later, the door swung open and a small, elderly woman stared up at him.

"Hello ma'am," Jeremy began. "Sorry to bother you. My truck's broken down and I need to get to the next town as soon as possible. My father's in the hospital there."

Jeremy knew he was chattering but didn't seem able to stop himself. "My father's had a heart attack and he's asking for me. Is there anyone here who could help me? If anyone has a spare fan belt, I'd be grateful. I'd be happy to pay for it. That's all I need and I'll be out of your way."

The woman nodded her head and gestured to Jeremy, inviting him inside. The young man could hear the music clearly enough to realize that a fiddle group was practicing Maritime jigs and reels.

The kitchen was warm and softly lit. It smelled like baking. Jeremy surprised himself by smiling. He looked out the kitchen window. The sky was darker than it had been. *Boy, I really am lucky that this woman's house was so close to where I broke down.*

Handing Jeremy a steaming mug of tea in one hand and a plate of warm sweet rolls in the other, the woman pushed open a swinging door at the opposite end of the kitchen. Jeremy followed her, juggling the welcome gift of food and drink. He found himself in a dimly lit room. *This looks like an old-fashioned parlour,* he thought as he sat down on a rough old brown sofa.

Jeremy nodded to the musicians, who were too involved in their music to bother nodding back at him. It would be rude to interrupt them to ask about getting some help with his truck, so he just took a welcome sip of tea and sat back on the couch before biting into one of the sweet rolls. Soon he was happily tapping his feet to the music.

The two young women and the young man in front of him looked so much alike that they had to be sisters and brother. The older man was likely their father and seemed to be the leader of the talented quartet. As one song ended, they began another. *Must've played together for so long that they know what's next,* Jeremy thought, enjoying the music and the musicians.

The tea was soothing and the rolls satisfying. Jeremy laid his head against the back of the couch. As he listened, the sound of the music changed just a bit. The lively tune the group had been playing now gave way to a quieter melody and then to the haunting strains of a gentle lament. Soon Jeremy fell fast asleep, dreaming of a day, a dozen years before when he and his father had hiked across a meadow and up a mountain slope.

The next thing he knew, Jeremy was awake. His first thought was that he felt rested and refreshed. His next thought, though, was that he was cold and uncomfortable. What had happened? He couldn't have been so rude as to fall asleep on some strangers' couch, could he? Unable to remember exactly what had happened, Jeremy opened his eyes.

What the heck? He scrambled to his feet and frantically looked around. It was light outside. He must not only have fallen asleep, but slept through the entire night. Weirder still, the room was empty, save for the couch.

Where's the rest of the furniture? Where's my tea mug and the plate? And the people? Where are they? Jeremy thought as he ran for the back door. A few minutes later, he was relieved to be back in his old truck.

Once he had caught his breath from the scare and the sprint, Jeremy tried not to think about what had just happened. Instead, he concentrated on what he needed to do to get the truck fixed. *I hope my Dad's all right,* he thought, realizing this was the first time since he'd wakened up that he'd felt concerned about his father rather than just about himself.

A rumbling sound in the distance interrupted Jeremy's thoughts. A dump truck was coming his way. He jumped out and flagged the driver down.

"Thanks for stopping!" he said.

"No problem, son," the older man replied. "Truck broken down?"

"The fan belt's snapped."

"Jump in and I'll give you a ride into town. Someone there'll be able to help you."

The two rode along in silence and Jeremy soon realized that he'd been wise the night before not to try walking to town. He never would've made it there before dark.

"Here we are," the driver said, extending his hand to shake Jeremy's. "There's a service station just over there."

"Thanks for the drive, sir," Jeremy said. "Lots of people would've driven right by."

"Maybe so, maybe so," the older man agreed. "But I stopped so you just make sure you always stop to help, too."

Jeremy nodded and jogged across the street to the service station.

"Hello?" he called out and listened to his own voice bounce around the cavernous old garage bay.

"I'll be right there," a muffled voice called from under the hood of a nearby car. "Go wait for me in the office."

"Okay," Jeremy replied and did as he was told. The place

was a mess. Yellowed, dusty papers were piled so high they were sliding over. The floor looked as though it hadn't been washed in years. A cluster of framed pictures hung on the wall above the cash register. The glass covering the pictures was thick with years of dirt and grease. One of the photographs was a hockey team and another was an old car, but it was the third one that caught Jeremy's eye.

Those are the musicians who were in that house! Jeremy realized with a start. *And that woman beside them, she's the lady who answered the door and gave me the tea and rolls.*

Jeremy was still staring at the picture in bewilderment when an overweight, middle-aged man appeared, wiping his hands on a rag.

"What can I do for ya, buddy?" he asked.

Jeremy swung around. He didn't know what to say. He knew he had to ask about the fan belt for his truck but his mind just wouldn't form those words. Instead, he pointed at the photograph and asked, "Who are those people?"

"That's the McNaughton family. Nicest people you'd ever care to meet and the finest musicians this area's ever produced. They played Maritime music, jigs and reels and such. They lived back down the road a piece," the man explained eyeing Jeremy a bit suspiciously.

"Lived?" Jeremy asked.

"Yeah. They're gone. It's a sad story. The whole lot of them died in a fire at the dancehall about ten years back. The family was completely wiped out."

The man lowered his voice and continued. "There wasn't even anyone to leave the house to. It's amazing that the old place is still standing. No one's been near it for years."

Silence hung in the air between the two men while the memory of ghostly music shivered down Jeremy's spine.

Pemaquid Point Lighthouse

The Pemaquid Point Lighthouse stands along the shoreline near Bristol, Maine. It's said that you can hear the mournful cries of the sailors who lost their lives when the sea hurled their ships against the rocks.

Occasionally, people report seeing the filmy image of a young woman walking near the water. Anyone who sees her knows immediately that she is not from this world, for she seems to be walking not on, but just above the rocks. Perhaps her pathetic soul is searching for the love of her earthly life. Perhaps he was one of the many sailors who have met their death against that shore.

A Hornet Nest of Phantoms

The aircraft carrier *USS Hornet* is now a museum, permanently docked at Alameda Point near San Francisco. The staff and volunteers are all experienced with ships and comfortable with their jobs. They're also not the kinds of people who are prone to wild flights of fantasy so when they talk of seeing apparitions, a wise ghost hunter will listen to what they have to say.

One day, the *Hornet's* marketing manager watched in amazement as an apparition dressed in an officer's uniform made his way toward the ship's engine room—and then, simply vanished.

Other employees report that ghosts seem to be constantly watching over them as they work. A few years ago in the month of December, several people watched in awe as the ghost of a sailor ran along the hangar deck and disappeared right into a Christmas tree! A thorough search of the premises determined that there was absolutely no one aboard the ship who shouldn't have been. Well, no one who was still alive, that is.

Other presences on the *Hornet* are only heard, not seen. After listening to footsteps nearby, people reasonably expect to find a flesh and blood person making the sounds. On the *Hornet* this is often not the case because those footsteps often pass by with no human being in sight.

Spookier still, are the phantom voices that can be heard deep in discussion even though those conversations took place years ago. Like the ghostly images that are seen, these voices may be examples of energy recorded in the environment, echoes of the past that provide witnesses with glimpses into yesterday.

Most of the manifestations aboard the *Hornet* seem completely unaware of today's world but one ghostly officer, in full uniform and making his way to the pilot house, actually acknowledges the living by making direct eye contact!

All those who've sensed the phantom presences aboard the *USS Hornet* agree that the spirits are helpful ones who must have had an association with the ship during their lifetimes and want the fine old aircraft carrier to have a successful "afterlife."

Phantom Warning

Georgetown, South Carolina, is one of the busiest ports on the Atlantic seaboard. Since 1801, a solitary lighthouse on North Island, near Georgetown, has guarded the spot where the waters of Winyah Bay mix with those of the Atlantic Ocean.

For many years, the North Island light was operated by a keeper and his young daughter. Occasionally the two rowed over to the mainland for supplies but the trip was treacherous so they had to wait until the waters were calm.

They'd kept to this routine for years. The keeper was able to do his work while making sure that his daughter had the material possessions she needed and at least some exposure to other people.

One day, when the pair left the island, the water was calm but before long a storm blew in. Within minutes, rain was pelting down on the tiny rowboat and its occupants. The girl bailed water out of the boat as fast as she could, but she was not able to keep up with the rain and waves pouring in. Her father pulled as hard as he could on the oars but the huge swells heaved the boat up and down and he was unable to make any headway.

Then a wave swept right over the flimsy rowboat and tossed the child into the angry sea. Her father jumped into the water after his daughter but he wasn't able to reach the child. He tried and tried until, just as she was sinking under the surface, he was able to grab hold of a piece of clothing.

After fighting the gale-force winds and the angry sea, the man had no energy left to lift either himself or his daughter into the rowboat. The best he could do was to cling to the side of his tiny craft.

And this was the pitiful sight that greeted the crew of a fishing vessel that sailed near the small boat. The fishermen performed an amazing rescue and, just before he lost consciousness, the man managed to mumble, "Thank you for saving my daughter and me," before passing out in the rescue boat.

The lighthouse keeper slept for hours but as soon as he woke up he wanted to see his child.

"You mentioned your daughter when we picked you up but you were alone. We figured you were just hallucinating."

"No, no!" the father screamed. "My daughter, she was with me. I must find her."

The fishermen tried but no one ever found the man's beloved daughter. His rescuers delivered him safely to his North Island home and, it is said, he never left there again.

Locals brought him any supplies he needed and, years later, he died alone in the lighthouse.

Even today, they say that when a storm hits, sailors see the pathetic image of a man and a little girl in a rowboat, battling the wind and waves as best they can. This supernatural sighting is always taken as a warning to sailors that a killer storm is building.

London Bridge

London Bridge is falling down, falling down, falling down,
London Bridge is falling down, my fair lady, oh!

That's what the nursery song would have us believe, anyway. Fortunately, the words of the jingle were never quite true, but by the 1960s the 250-year-old bridge was steadily sinking into England's River Thames. Of course, a sinking bridge is not very safe so London Bridge was closed. Then the people in charge wondered what to do next. Making the bridge safe again was impossible and demolishing it wasn't an option either because London Bridge was a world-famous landmark.

Ideas were proposed and discussed until one enterprising soul made an absolutely ridiculous suggestion. "Let's sell London Bridge!"

What utter nonsense! Who on earth would buy a sinking bridge? Well, believe it or not, someone did. A man named Robert McCulloch actually bought the famous old structure.

But what would McCulloch do with London Bridge, especially since he lived thousands of miles away in Arizona, a state famous for its deserts? What could anyone possibly do with a bridge in a desert?

Well, it turns out that Robert McCulloch had a plan and he was anxious to show the world exactly what could be done with a bridge in a desert. London Bridge would not "fall down," it would be *taken* down.

Piece by piece, English workers took the bridge apart. They numbered each piece carefully so that the workers in Arizona would know how each brick and stone fit together in place. By the time the job was complete, there was no London Bridge left, just ships full of old, carefully packed, bridge-building material.

Once the ships had made their long voyage from Britain to America, they docked at Long Beach, California, which, by coincidence, is also where the very haunted British ship the *Queen Mary* is permanently docked. From Long Beach, workers transferred the important cargo to trucks that would take the disassembled bridge to its final destination—Lake Havasu in western Arizona.

Many people laughed at Robert McCulloch's crazy and expensive plan but in the end it was a winner. Workers reassembled the bridge like an enormous jigsaw puzzle using the numbers written on the bricks. The entire job took four years.

While the workers were busy rebuilding the bridge,

other people were also busy in the area. By the time the elegant old bridge stretched across the Arizona lake, an entire English village had been built beside it. McCulloch had created a unique tourist attraction complete with double-decker buses, bright red English "call boxes" (we know them as phone booths), pubs and fish-and-chips shops. Now North Americans could experience a bit of Britain without leaving their continent.

In October 1971, the exhibit officially opened. The crowd that had gathered for the ceremony watched as four people dressed in old-fashioned British clothing walked slowly across London Bridge. Most folks simply assumed that the people in the costumes were actors hired to remind everyone of the famous landmark's heritage. But no actors had been hired to perform that day.

It wasn't until those people in old-fashioned clothing vanished before the crowd's eyes that the situation became clear. Robert McCulloch had succeeded in importing much more than just the mortar and bricks of London Bridge. He had also unknowingly brought along some of the many ghosts that were known to haunt various parts of London, England.

Today, London Bridge remains a successful tourist attraction. It also remains haunted. The ghosts on the bridge seem completely unaware of their modern American surroundings. They simply stroll along peacefully in their afterlife until they slowly vaporize, only to stroll again another day as they have been doing for centuries.

The House That Ghosts Built

What has 160 rooms, 47 fireplaces, 40 bedrooms, 13 bathrooms, 5 kitchens, 2 basements, lots of secret passageways, staircases that lead nowhere and more than 2000 doors, including some that open into thin air? Oh, and the place was thought to be haunted with hundreds and hundreds of ghosts

There is only one correct answer to that question and that is the Winchester House in San Jose, California.

Sarah Winchester, whose family invented the Winchester rifle in the 1860s, built the enormous home. Sarah believed that her house was haunted by the spirits of all the people who had been killed by the popular rifle. She was sure that their souls were angry with her and so she tried to hide from them by sleeping in a different bedroom every night. Oddly, she felt safe from supernatural attacks during the day, as long as she never finished building the house. As a result, the house was always under construction. The place got bigger every year from 1884 when Sarah bought the land, until 1922 when she died. By then the mansion was an enormous confusing maze!

At night, to appease the ghosts, Sarah Winchester had her servants bring 13 expensive meals to the dining room table at midnight. Then Sarah would ring a bell to invite 12 different ghost-guests to join her. After the meal, the servants would clear the plates (and probably enjoy the food that the ghosts hadn't eaten) while Sarah played the piano or the organ for hours so that the ghosts could dance! This strange routine went on for nearly 40 years.

Today, Winchester House is a major tourist attraction. Ghost hunters have an especially good time in the house because the bizarre building is still haunted but these days it's Sarah's ghost who is the most active. She's been heard playing tunes on the organ, in rooms where there's never been an organ. People have even recorded the phantom music.

When Sarah's ghost is seen it's is said to be so life-like that people think they've seen a real person dressed in old-fashioned clothing, that is until she disappears before their eyes! Other times, people can hear someone breathing and whispering but they can't see anyone near them. Cold drafts and strange balls of light, both of which are common signs that a house is haunted, are often felt or seen throughout the house.

The clear image of a man dressed in overalls once turned up in a photograph taken at Winchester House even though no one other than the photographer was in the room when the picture was taken! No one knows for certain who that man was in life but it's likely he was one of the hundreds of workers Sarah hired to build her bizarre mansion.

If you visit Winchester House during one of the daytime tours and you don't get spooked enough then you can always try one of the special night-time tours that include lots of eerie areas that people don't normally get to see. And really, you might as well, because it would be a shame to visit the world's largest haunted house without at least saying "hello" to the long-dead Sarah Winchester!

Ghost Stories of the White House

One of the most famous houses in the world is at 1600 Pennsylvania Avenue, in Washington, D.C.—the White House. This stately mansion has been the home to United States presidents since 1800. And it has been haunted for almost all of that time.

When John Adams, the second president of the United States, and his wife, Abigail moved into the White House the building was still under construction. Perhaps that is why Abigail's ghost has been seen drifting through closed doors on her way to hang the presidential laundry up to dry in the East Wing.

Dolley Madison, whose husband was the fourth president, returned to the White House nearly a century after her death. Dolley's ghost scolded a gardener who was about to dig up rose bushes that she had planted long, long ago when she was First Lady. The startled gardener wisely agreed to leave Mrs. Madison's treasured roses where they were. No one has ever tried to rearrange the White House rose garden since.

Not far from those rose bushes, the soul of a soldier, dressed in a uniform from the War of 1812 between Britain and the United States, wanders the grounds. Perhaps he's still guarding the White House—or maybe the rose bushes!

And two other ghosts also haunt the beautiful lawns around the mansion. In life, both men worked there. They were apparently so devoted to their jobs that they have chosen to stay at work forever.

Even some former presidents haunt the presidential mansion. In the 1930s, Andrew Jackson was heard laughing in the Rose Room and he had been dead for nearly 100 years by then. Thomas Jefferson has been heard practicing his violin, even though he's been dead since 1826.

President William Harrison only lived in the White House for a month before he died in April 1841. Judging by the ghostly encounters people have had with his presence, it's pretty clear that he managed to hang around the official residence much longer in death than he did in life. Oddly enough this phantom is most often seen and heard in the White House attic.

But the ghost of Abraham Lincoln is the wraith who's encountered most often. Lincoln held office from 1861 until his assassination in 1865. His tall, thin, bearded image usually appears in times of trouble. During World War II, for instance, Queen Wilhelmina of the Netherlands stayed overnight at the White House. At bedtime, the queen heard a knock at her bedroom door. She opened the door and there, before her eyes, stood the ghost of President Abraham Lincoln! No wonder she fainted dead away.

At breakfast the next morning, Queen Wilhelmina told President and Mrs. Roosevelt about her eerie visitor. First Lady Eleanor Roosevelt was not surprised. She had sensed Lincoln's presence herself many times and had also noticed that their pet dog would sometimes bark at something that only the animal could see.

When Winston Churchill was the prime minister of Britain, he also stayed at the White House overnight. He asked to be moved to another bedroom after he saw Abraham Lincoln's sad-looking ghost staring out the window of the first room he had been given.

A secretary working at the White House handled an encounter with Lincoln quite calmly. She passed the open door of a bedroom and saw Lincoln's ghost sitting on the bed pulling his boots on. The secretary merely continued on her errand.

Those haunted rooms were renovated in 1952, and Lincoln's spirit has not been seen as often since then. But even today, there are still people who speak in hushed tones when the topic of ghosts in the White House is mentioned.

Famous Phantom Train

It was twilight, that in-between time that is neither day nor night. Thirteen-year-old Jim glanced at his watch. 7:20. He'd have to head home soon.

It's so cold, the boy thought as he sat on the top ledge of a frosty wooden fence. *It's April but it feels more like winter.* Jim pumped his legs back and forth at a steady pace and crossed his arms over his chest to try to keep his long, lanky body warm. Despite being uncomfortably chilly, Jim enjoyed being by himself, outside, at one of his favourite places.

The fence along the south boundary of his family's farm was near the railroad and Jim loved to stare along the empty miles of tracks. The view made him feel that the whole world stretched out endlessly before him and breathing in the crisp, unseasonably cold air sharpened his thinking. Maybe he'd plan his batting strategy for the next baseball game.

The boy checked his watch for a second time and eased

himself down from his perch. *It's wicked how cold it is out here*, he thought. *I'd better get home.*

Just as Jim was about to take his first step, an unfamiliar sensation stopped him. Was it a muffled sound nearby or a perhaps a movement way off in the distance? As he paused to look and listen, the damp cold surrounded him. Thick pillows of gray fog rose from the ground and dark clouds blocked out the thin ribbon of moonlight. Within seconds, Jim was wrapped in silent, murky blackness. Everything he counted on in his world was gone. He was beyond frightened.

It's so dark. Pitch black and way too quiet, like something's sucked out every bit of light and sound in the world, Jim thought.

A cold, hard shudder snaked down the boy's backbone. The coppery taste of panic filled the back of his throat. *I can't even see the train tracks.* He tried to flee toward the warmth and safety of home but his feet would not budge. *Fog can't paralyze a person, can it?*

The dark, silent stillness hung about him for just a moment longer. Then, through the thick blanket of fog, he saw something even darker: a solid black shape moving toward him along the train tracks. Seconds later, an old-fashioned steam engine emerged from the fog.

This can't be real, Jim thought. *Those engines are only in museums and besides trains make noise, lots of noise.*

But the train kept coming. The engine was at least twice

as big as any Jim had ever seen before and it was covered with black cloth that fluttered like flags on a blustery day.

He glanced down at the tracks; tracks that he thought he knew so well. Much to his horror, the boy saw that those tracks had changed. They were no longer made of steel. Instead, this unnatural train was traveling over a black carpet spread endlessly out in front of it.

Looking up again, Jim found he could see inside the train cars as they rolled past him. Right behind the locomotive was another huge railcar. It too was draped in black cloth and utterly silent. Inside, a group of soldiers stood at attention around a table. They wore old-fashioned uniforms and looked not quite life-like. Atop the table lay a coffin.

The railcar following carried an orchestra. The musicians all wore black and, they were ever so slightly transparent.

The train rolled past Jim in deadly silence.

This can't be happening.

But it was.

As Jim watched the supernatural vision slowly and silently disappear into the distance the air began to clear. *The train is taking the fog with it,* he thought.

In an instant, Jim's world returned to normal. He sighed with relief as he found that he was able to move once again. *I'd better get home. It must be really late and I sure can't tell Mom that I was watching a ghost train pass by.*

The boy looked at his watch; it was eight minutes *before* the phantom train came through the fog! *But that's impossi-*

ble, Jim thought. *That train took at least twenty minutes to pass.*

Or so it seemed.

An icicle of terror dripped down Jim's spine. He sprinted away from the tracks as fast as his frightened legs would carry him.

Once he was safely inside, the house seemed an especially warm and welcoming place that night. He had no idea what he'd encountered down at the railroad tracks; he was just relieved that the strange experience had ended and that he was safely back home.

What a shame that young Jim hadn't known that he had witnessed one of the world's most famous and enduring ghostly events; President Abraham Lincoln's phantom funeral train; the apparition of the train that had carried the president's body back to his home in Springfield, Illinois in April 1865.

Every April, along the route that the slain president's funeral train actually traveled those many, many years ago, there are reports of supernatural images like the one Jim witnessed. So many people have seen President Lincoln's phantom train that the spectral spectacle has been reported in newspapers and magazines around the world.

Even on the warmest day, the air around the track gets cold and the sky darkens. Then the steam engine, with long black streamers, pulling railcars of slightly transparent musicians all dressed in black, and, of course, Lincoln's casket, passes noiselessly by.

If the night is moonlit, clouds always drift through the sky to cover the moon and all is silent. Witnesses say they can see the musicians playing their instruments but that the music seems frozen. If the wind is blowing, a calm settles and there is a solemn hush overall. Clocks and watches always stop until the procession has passed. Then they are found to be five to eight minutes slow.

But what of the silence? Surely that is impossible, trains make noise, at least normal trains do. But this phantom train apparently travels under a dome of supernatural silence.

The only day all year this ghostly phenomenon is ever seen is on April 20 and only on train tracks that run along the route that President Lincoln's funeral train traveled in 1865.

Up on the Roof

Judging by the number of stories about haunted houses, maybe having a ghost in a house isn't all that unusual. But having a ghost on a house is definitely a bit odd. Even so there was a ghost on the roof of a house in the southern United States that only appeared in the evenings during the month of December. For years the wraith would show up the moment the clock ticked off the last second of November 30th and he'd stay until the very second the New Year arrived.

No one knows what the entity did during the daytime in December, or where he was for the rest of the year. For that matter, no one knew why the ghost appeared on the roof when he did or even why he disappeared when he did but they were certain that the apparition came from the past because he was dressed in old-fashioned clothes including spats and a top hat.

It's too bad that people didn't think to talk to an elderly lady in the nearby seniors' home because she knew precisely whose spirit was pacing back and forth along the roof and even why he was there.

It seems that on December 1, 1932, a group of young men found the house empty and decided to make it their temporary home. Times were tough then, during the Great Depression and few people had a decent place to live; even fewer had jobs and almost no one had enough money. These young men had come to town on a promise of work but, when they arrived, there were no jobs to be found. What they did find, though, was this empty house.

Young men being what they are—money or no money, jobs or no jobs—they liked to have fun. One night, one of the fellows found some fancy clothes to dress up in. Then, perhaps on a dare, he went up on the roof and walked back and forth, calling out to his friends below. They all enjoyed the stunt until the lad lost his balance and toppled to his death.

Terrified that they would be blamed, the others quickly left town the next day and were never seen again. But their dead friend's ghost came back every December to offer a permanent reminder the Dirty Thirties killed another healthy, ambitious young man.

Horrors in Amityville

Have you ever watched that scary old movie called *Amityville Horror*? Of course, it's only scary if you believe that the story is true and that those supernatural events actually occurred. By now, it's almost impossible to know whether to believe the tale or not. Read on and then decide for yourself.

The gruesome, unnatural encounters in the stately three-storey home began in 1974, when a deranged man named Ronald Defeo murdered his entire family as they slept in the house. When Defeo was arrested for his terrible crime, he told police that the murders were not his fault. He claimed that ghostly voices had ordered him to kill. After hearing that account, people agreed that Ronald Defeo was a very sick and dangerous man. To protect everyone from further harm, he was locked away.

The house stood empty for a time but then George and Kathleen Lutz and their three children moved into the place. The Lutz family thought that this would be their home for years to come. Sadly, that was not the case. All five of them fled in the middle of the night, just four weeks after they'd moved in. During their 28 days in the house, the Lutzes said that they had endured dozens of terrifying paranormal encounters.

Right from the day they moved in, everyone in the family heard heavy phantom footsteps thumping throughout empty parts of the house. There were strange pockets of air, sometimes hot, sometimes cold, that floated about for reasons no one in the family could understand and windows broke when no one was near them when they broke.

Not long after that, the Lutzes began to notice horrible smells in the house. Sometimes the living room would smell so absolutely terrible that no one could stand to be in there. Then, as suddenly as the foul odour had come, it would leave, hideously turning up another day in another room.

Soon the house seemed to take on a life of its own. Green slime oozed from cracks in the walls and from the ceilings. Black goo dripped from door handles.

Nothing the Lutzes did could stop the mess or even clean it. Then, much to their terrified disgust, swarms of flies invaded the house; and then flew away, back into the great beyond as mysteriously as they had appeared!

It's hard to believe that anyone could live in such a haunted house but the Lutzes swore they did exactly that.

The situation was even worse for the children because with each day they stood by helplessly as their parents changed into people they didn't even recognize. Kathleen's face became twisted and ugly. George grew a beard and took on a look that his family had never seen before. Whatever possessed the house was now trying to possess the people living there.

When a pair of evil-looking red eyes floated freely around the rooms, the family knew that something had to be done. They contacted a priest who tried to bless the house to clear it of the dreadful spirits but he couldn't perform the blessing. He was driven away by inhuman voices ordering him to leave.

Later that same week, the Lutz family realized they couldn't take the strain of living in such a haunted house any longer and they fled in the middle of the night, vowing never to return.

The Amityville story might have ended then and there except that a writer named Jay Anson heard about this most haunted of houses. He decided to write a book describing all the eerie events the family had endured. Anson had just begun to work on the story when two terrifying events occurred in his life. Although he'd always been a very healthy person, Anson suddenly had a heart attack. Then his son was in a terrible car accident. It seemed that the evil in the house was spreading out beyond its walls.

When Anson phoned the priest who'd tried to bless the house, he was told that the man had become critically ill shortly after visiting the house in Amityville.

Then a filmmaker, ignoring this dreadful run of "bad luck" for anyone associated with the haunted house, foolishly decided the story would make a good movie. That was just as bad an idea as Anson's book had been. Actors hired to play roles in the movie suddenly suffered strange accidents. On the first day of filming, James Brolin, who was playing the role of George Lutz, was trapped in a hotel elevator for nearly an hour and the next morning he tripped on a camera cable and sprained his ankle.

Then, once the movie was made and showing in theaters, the people involved in the film began arguing and even suing each other. It seemed that the evil spirits in the house would stop at nothing to have people leave them alone. Unfortunately, no one was wise enough to be mindful of those angry, ghostly messages.

Eventually, the haunting calmed down. That house in Amityville, once filled with horror, still stands but today it is a normal, peaceful home. The new owners claim that there is nothing unusual about the house by now.

And that is the end of the Amityville horror story, except for one other fact that you might be interested in. Long before that house was built, Native Americans living in the area would not go near that piece of land. They said it was home to evil spirits.

It's hard to believe that a piece of land could be so haunted for so long that it caused all this trouble over the years but then it's even harder to believe that anyone could make up such a story!

Trailer Tale

The week that his parents separated, Matt's life went seriously downhill. He and his mother, Cindy, moved out of the apartment where the 13-year-old and his parents had always lived and into the first place they could find; a shabby, old two-bedroom mobile home in a trailer park. Even though Cindy tried to fix it up, their new home was dreadful. It seemed to Matt that his life couldn't possibly get any worse but he was wrong about that.

His life was about to get much worse because that trailer was very haunted.

In the middle of the first night in the trailer, Matt jolted awake. He glanced at his clock. It was 3:23. For just an instant he wondered what had wakened him. Then he remembered. He had heard someone come into his room. Matt sat up in bed, rubbed his eyes and looked around the small room.

"Mom?" he said quietly, hoping he would hear his

mother's voice assuring him that everything was all right. But there was no answer.

Matt tried to tell himself that he was just hearing things. But he knew he wasn't. There was someone in his room. He could hear rhythmic, raspy breathing and it wasn't his own. He lay awake for the rest of the night.

The next morning, Cindy commented on how tired Matt looked. He didn't want to tell her that something he couldn't see had been in his room during the night. She had enough on her mind right now.

During the day, Matt tried to convince himself that he just wasn't used to the new, strange sounds of the trailer at night. But it didn't work because deep down, he knew exactly what he had heard. Someone or something had been in the tiny, dark bedroom with him.

The boy also knew that he was never going to be able to sleep in that room again so he told his mother that he wanted to fall asleep watching TV in the living room. Unfortunately, just after he fell asleep, he was startled awake by the sound of a telephone ringing.

What the heck? He thought as he jumped from the couch, bumping his shin on the coffee table as he reached for the telephone. He mumbled "hello" in a groggy voice, but there was no reply. The ringing sound continued. *That sound's not coming from the phone*, the boy thought. *It's coming from my bedroom.* But there was no phone in his room. Matt was wide awake now, his heart was pounding hard. He bolted toward his bedroom.

Cindy was standing at the door of her own bedroom. Together they went into his room. The ringing stopped. All was quiet; so quiet that Matt could hear the breathing sounds again. He looked at his mother to see if she was also hearing them but she just stared straight ahead and looked confused.

"It isn't really the telephone ringing, Mom. I checked," Matt said quietly.

His mother just nodded. Silently they walked to the living room.

"Let's turn on some lights," Cindy suggested. But the glare from the lamps made strange shadow on the walls, so they turned them off again and waited fearfully in the dark until the sun came up.

Finally, when it was light outside, Matt's mother made breakfast. "This is going to be even tougher than we thought it would be," she said sadly.

Matt just nodded.

Through the day, the pair acted as though nothing had happened. They worked together to finish unpacking and hanging pictures. That evening as they sat down to dinner, Matt's mother asked him if he was feeling all right.

"Just tired," he replied.

"You don't look well, Matt," she said quietly.

The boy laughed for the first time in days. "No kidding!"

he said loudly. "You don't look so great yourself, you know, Mom. You're as pale as a ghost."

The words were no sooner out of Matt's mouth than heavy footsteps began to echo from the back of the trailer. It sounded as though someone was pacing between the bedrooms. Matt and his mother stared at one another in disbelief. They knew they were the only flesh-and-blood people inside the trailer at that moment. They also knew for certain now that the place was haunted.

Cindy stood up. "We're going to have to find another place to live, Matt."

They both understood that an angry entity did not want them there. They grabbed their jackets, got into the car and headed for a motel. If the phantom wanted that trailer so badly, he or she or it could have it.

Several days later, once they'd found an apartment, Cindy and Matt drove back to the trailer. They were both nervous as Cindy steered the car into the parking space. Neither of them made a move to get out. They couldn't. They were frozen in fear.

A piercing pair of disembodied eyes stared menacingly at them from the nearest window. Cindy backed the car up as fast as she could. "Whatever that evil spirit might be, we have to leave it in peace. We can hire a moving company to go in and get our stuff. Maybe the thing will have calmed down by then."

And that is exactly what they did.

Matt and Cindy enjoyed "camping out" in their apartment while they waited for the movers to empty the haunted trailer. By the time summer holidays came around that year, the pair had almost forgotten their horrible nights there.

An Old Haunt

You might not want to live in a haunted house but visiting one could be fun! Take for instance, Liberty Hall in Frankfort, Kentucky. This beautiful mansion was built in 1796 as the home for one of Kentucky's first senators John Brown and his family. Brown's descendants continued to live in the grand old place until 1955. Today, the home's a museum where the public is welcome. Better still, the museum's staff embrace the fact that their venue is haunted.

The ghost is known as the Gray Lady and some say that in life she was Mrs. Brown's aunt, Margaret Varick. If this is so, then her story is a double tragedy.

In 1817, after the Brown's child died, Margaret traveled nearly a thousand miles, by horse drawn carriage and on horseback, to comfort the bereaved parents. Sadly the trip was too much for Aunt Margaret and she died just a few days after arriving at Liberty Hall.

The earliest recorded sighting of the ghost was in the 1820s when the Browns' grandson watched a gray form moving about the second floor of the stately home. The spirit was seen again by a great-grandchild in the 1880s and even today her image is still occasionally seen, and often sensed.

The description of the ghost is always the same, a filmy shape, dressed in a gray dress, floating just slightly above the floor. She's been seen attending to chores around the house and sometimes simply staring out a window, perhaps taking a break. Even though time has marched on for the outside world, it would seem that everything in the Gray Lady's afterlife has stayed exactly the same. If you do visit Liberty Hall, don't forget to pay your respects.

Time and Again

The word "precognition" means sensing that something will occur in the future. You might wonder how can anyone know about something before it's even happened. One possibility might be that, just as there are ghosts from the past, there may also be ghosts from the future. "Retrocognition" means the opposite of precognition. Retrocognition is the supernatural experience of seeing something as it was in the past.

An excellent example of retrocognition occurred some sixty years ago in Vancouver, a city on Canada's west coast, when a young woman we'll call Carol went into her favourite department store. She walked down the stairs to the store's lower level. As she reached the bottom step, she was shocked at what she saw. The store had changed into an old-fashioned shop. Customers and store clerks wearing clothes that were in style in the 19th century walked about chatting with one another. Even the merchandise was old fashioned.

Buckets of grain and barrels of oats stood on a worn wooden floor.

Fascinated and a bit frightened, the young woman stood still as these old-fashioned people moved about, choosing things to buy. Although Carol couldn't hear their voices, she could see that they were talking to one another. The supernatural spectacle played out for several minutes and then faded away. Seconds later, the store looked exactly like the one she was familiar with.

What on earth had happened in those few minutes? Did Carol lose her senses? Probably not. It's more likely she experienced that special kind of supernatural sighting known as retrocognition, a mysterious glimpse back in time.

Road Wraith

Nancy and her parents were driving home from the restaurant where they'd been celebrating Nancy's thirteenth birthday. The meal had been excellent and everyone in the family was in a happy mood. The night was clear and crisp. The full moon shone and there was little traffic on the roads. As Nancy's mother drove, they chatted about the fun they'd had and their plans for the weekend.

They were driving through an intersection a few blocks from the restaurant, when suddenly Nancy's father let out a yell. Nancy jerked her head around to see what the problem was. Then she screamed too, even louder than her father had, but Nancy's scream was drowned out by the sound of their car's tires skidding on the pavement. Her mother was almost standing on the brake pedal, her face white with fear as a small black car sped across the road. It seemed to be heading straight for them. Bracing themselves for a crash, the family held their collective breath until they realized that the other car had missed theirs by a few inches.

"That idiot!" Nancy's father exclaimed. "He didn't even notice the stop sign."

The family's happy mood was gone. Nancy's father shook his fist angrily at the dangerous driver who'd nearly hit them. Making rude gestures to bad drivers is never a safe thing to do, but the man was not thinking clearly.

It was a few moments before Nancy's mother felt calm enough to continue driving. She inched across the rest of the intersection slowly and cautiously. They'd driven less than a block when the same small black car appeared again —right beside their car! The troublemaker at the wheel pulled his vehicle up close and waved to get the frightened family's attention. He certainly succeeded because this was not a sight either Nancy or her parents would ever forget. The driver was not a person. The driver was a skeleton! It stared menacingly at them through empty eye sockets before unlocking its jawbone to laugh madly and silently at the terrified family. "Lock your door!" Nancy's mother ordered as she concentrated on driving away from the evil black car with its dead driver. No matter how fast she drove though, the miserable manifestation stayed right beside them!

Finally, almost too terrified to think at all, Nancy's mother called out, "Brace yourselves" before yanking the steering wheel sharply to the right. Unfortunately, fear had erased her judgment and their car smashed hard into the curb.

Now at least they were stopped, but their car had a flat tire and a mangled fender. The terrified family took a moment to look around for the deadly driver who had caused the accident but the street was deserted.

"That's ridiculous," Nancy's father mumbled. "He couldn't have driven away from us that quickly. His car was right beside ours just a second ago."

"Forget about the stupid car," her mother said quietly and wisely. "So long as it's gone, I'm happy. Who cares where or how it got away? We're lucky that all we need is a tow truck, not an ambulance. Or a hearse."

By the time the tow truck arrived, Nancy and her parents had climbed out of their car and were leaning against its fender. They stood up straight and moved toward the tow-truck driver as he got out of his truck.

"How did you manage this?" the tow-truck driver asked.

Nancy's father replied, "You're not going to believe this, it's going to sound crazy but a maniac driver with the best skeleton costume I've ever seen is to blame for this."

For a moment the tow-truck driver just stared at them. Then he spoke. "You must mean the phantom car. I can hardly believe it. As far as I know, no one's seen that evil thing for years. That's no costume the driver's wearing. That's him. He's a skeleton, a phantom skeleton. His car's a phantom too. The folks around here call it the car from hell."

He walked around the car, assessing the damage. "From

all I've heard, I guess they have good reason to call it that. Listen, I think you can drive your car if we just change the tire. If you want, I can tell you the legend while I'm changing the tire for you." Nancy tucked herself in between her parents as they moved to the front of their car.

"Hand me a wrench," the tow-truck driver said pointing to a toolbox he'd set down at the curb. "I'll have this flat changed and you'll be on your way again in a few minutes."

"Not until you explain what just happened," Nancy reminded him.

"Oh yes, the phantom car," the man said as he went right to work. "They say it was first seen about 25 years ago, the very night that they pulled a small black car up from the bottom of the harbour. The police said the car must have been under the water for months—with the driver's body still in it. They said that it looked as though the fish had fed on every bit of flesh the man ever had. According to the news, there was nothing left of him at all. Nothing except his bones, that is."

The tow-truck driver stood up, wiped his hands on a rag that he'd had in his pocket and began to pick up the tools he'd used for change the damaged tire.

"For years afterward, the image of that car and its driver were seen around here, but you two are the first folks I've heard about in years who've seen it. Guess you found out why they call it the car from hell."

After paying the man for changing the tire, the exhausted family got back into the car and drove home in silence. The only time they spoke was when they agreed not to mention their supernatural encounter with the phantom car to anyone. Ever. And they didn't.

Hopefully Nancy and her family never visited Bachelor's Grove Cemetery, near Chicago, Illinois. Phantom cars and even phantom trucks are regularly seen driving near the graveyard. Most of the ghostly vehicles look as though they're from the 1930s. People say that these phantoms are ghosts of cars and trucks once owned by some of Chicago's worst gangsters.

So, next time you're out driving with your parents, or even crossing the street, don't be too sure that the cars you're seeing are real—they might be road wraiths.

The Haunted Ladies

Hearses—those big dignified vehicles that carry coffins—are very special cars. They're even more luxurious than limousines. Unfortunately, most of us don't get a chance to ride in a hearse until it's way too late to enjoy the experience. But at least one company owns two hearses that they use to drive living people. Best of all for ghost hunters, those drives go to and from some of the most haunted places in the world.

The company is Destiny Tours and the haunted places they visit are in Sydney, Australia. The funky old hearses are both Cadillacs. One is named Elvira, the other, Morticia. Both of these gorgeous "old ladies," as their owner calls them, are very haunted. They're so haunted that they each have a distinct personality. Now that's not something that you can say about most cars, is it?

Elvira is a 1967 model and she does not like people standing near her front. She asks them to move by making them feel so uncomfortable that they finally walk around to her side or back. Morticia, a rare 1962 model, is not air-conditioned but even so, on steamy hot nights, cool breezes blow about inside her even when her windows are rolled up tight.

There is so much ghostly activity in and around these cars that owner Allan Levinson records it all in a logbook.

Allan always knew there was something quite supernatural about his beloved hearses. He invited Debbie Malone, a well-known Australian psychic, to visit the cars. She revealed that the presence haunting Elvira had gone to the spirit world at about the same time as the car was manufactured.

Who could it be?

It didn't take long to find out.

Debbie rode in each car during their tours and came away without any doubts. She began by announcing, "Morticia and Elvira are definitely haunted." She must have seen the ghost in Elvira because she said he was a man who wears glasses, a white shirt, black suit and occasionally a hat. She even knew his name: Tom.

In all likelihood, Tom was a funeral director who would have driven the hearse when the car was new. If passengers are ever so impolite as to make fun of either Tom or Elvira, they always regret it because such foolish jokesters come down with an upset stomach. Now that's a ghostly lesson in manners!

Most people, not just psychics or pranksters, feel

something out of the ordinary in the car. Sometimes riders sense Tom's spirit as a dignified, well-dressed man who is very fond of the car. Other times, he makes himself known to passengers as a puzzling pocket of very cold air that floats about the car. Children are generally much better at sensing ghosts than adults are and so it wasn't much of a shock to a tour driver when an eight-year-old girl saw the cold spot as a circle white light moving around in the car.

Morticia has a very different personality, probably because she was not just a hearse but an ambulance too so, in addition to carrying dead bodies, she also carried people who were gravely ill and others who were dying.

Like Elvira, Morticia is also haunted by the phantom of a man. Another psychic determined that the ghost's name is Bill McGowan and he was a smoker when he was alive. He usually appears sitting in the driver's seat.

As Elvira and Morticia travel around their spooky routes, the rides can get very "spirited," because other ghosts sometimes join them for at least part of the trip. When the tours stop at the old Darlinghurst Gaol (jail) for instance, passengers occasionally feel a strange tightness around their throats. There have been many hangings at that jail over the years and that may explain that uncomfortable choking feeling.

Another stop on the tour is a former orphanage. Here people often smell roses in the cars, even though there are no flowers anywhere near the grand old hearses. After a bit of research, the mystery of the beautiful smell was solved. It seems that an area of the orphanage is haunted by the ghost of a woman who, when she was alive, loved rose-scented perfume.

After visiting one haunted building, some tourists settled back into Elvira once again. Seconds later, one of those people clearly saw three shadows when there were only two people present at the time. Someone, or something, had obviously decided to tag along for a ride. Another time, a soul from the Woronora Cemetery popped into the hearse after the tour had driven away from his body's earthly resting place.

Many folks on these spooky tours take pictures during the drives. It seems that the spirits enjoy messing with people's cameras and phones. Sometimes their cameras will simply stop working for a while and then, just as suddenly will start working again perfectly well. Perhaps those in their afterlife don't play with anything for too long before they move on to some other trick.

When the cameras and phones do function, the pictures people take often show round, white dots scattered about. It's believed that these dots, usually called "orbs," are a type of ghostly manifestation.

Allan Levinson explained that, "on every tour someone will feel something." So it's possible that while you've been reading about them, the two haunted hearses were showing their passengers a supernaturally good time!

Dread 107

Not one railroad engineer in Colorado ever wanted to drive the locomotive with the number 107 painted on its side. The railroaders agreed among themselves that the engine was jinxed. And it's no wonder there was such talk because even when it was new, that locomotive caused nothing but trouble for anyone who drove it; or tried to drive it.

An engineer named Duncan swore that it was the locomotive, and not him, that tried to cross a bridge that had been washed out by heavy rains the week before. What a catastrophe. The engineer, the locomotive, the train behind it and everyone aboard went straight into the flooded river.

At first, the other railroad workers were sure that Duncan was just making excuses for himself. Sometime later however, another engineer driving the 107 struck a boulder that had fallen on the track. It wasn't that this engineer had been careless. He'd seen the boulder and had tried to stop the train, but locomotive 107 simply kept moving until it crashed into the enormous rock. Soon after that incident, railroad employees began to refer to the troublesome engine as "Dread 107," for they all dreaded having to drive it.

Three months after the collision with the boulder, "Dread" drove itself into an avalanche of snow. The company that owned this terrible and devilish piece of railroad equipment finally gave up and scrapped it once and for all.

That was when the ghost of the evil engine appeared.

For years after it was demolished, people reported seeing the glow of Dread 107's headlight off in the distance and hearing the familiar shrill pitch of its whistle, despite the fact that the tracks on which it once traveled no longer existed! Even demolition, it seemed, could not destroy the evil spirit that possessed the locomotive with the number 107 painted on its side.

Phantom Ships

Some of the most intriguing ghostly phenomena are phantom ships; apparitions of ships that sailed the world's waterways long, long ago. These ghost ships are often called a *Flying Dutchman* in honour of an ancient legend about a vessel that sank off the southern tip of Africa. It's said that the ship's captain was a bully who worked his sailors too hard and often risked their lives by sailing into danger.

As this cruel captain was guiding his ship through the treacherous waters around the Cape of Good Hope a vicious storm blew up. Hurricane-force winds ripped the ship's sails to shreds and enormous waves pounded her gunnels and washed over her deck. Terrified, the crew pleaded with their captain to turn back but the man insisted that they sail on.

The sailors knew their lives were in peril so they overpowered the captain and threw his body into the churning sea below. A moment later, an enormous green wave swamped the *Flying Dutchman's* deck, splintering the wooden ship into bits. The men's lives were over in an instant but their wretched and eternal afterlives had only begun.

Over the centuries, hundreds of people, even Britain's King George V, have seen the image of that ill-fated ship battling through violent ocean storms. Some witnesses even report seeing the ghosts of those long-dead sailors frantically working with the vessel's ropes and sails, fighting eternally, and hopelessly, to keep their ship afloat.

Sailors are a superstitious lot with long memories and seeing a phantom ship is considered a seriously bad omen, said to cause swift and sure death to any who see such a mirage. As a result, there is a rich enough collection of such tales to keep curious fans of the supernatural captivated for years. Some of these stories are well known. Others, like the following tales, are so frightening to seafarers that they are rarely told.

In 1870, a British schooner called the *Daphne* set out on a voyage across the Pacific to a destination near Australia where, they'd been told, a schooner had struck a reef and sunk into an underwater cave. The sunken ship, people said, had been carrying a huge cargo of gold and jewels. Whoever salvaged the treasure would be rich beyond imagination. The *Daphne's* owners and crew were determined to find the wreck and claim the fortune.

Once they reached the site, the sailors lost no time organizing their best swimmers into an underwater search party. The rest of the crew stayed on the *Daphne's* deck while others climbed the mast as lookouts to watch for ships that might also be searching for the treasure.

Before long, a sailor, perched on the highest part of the *Daphne's* mast, spotted another ship on the horizon. The craft seemed to be sailing toward them, so the sailor called out an alert. The crew armed themselves in case they had to fight to protect the gold they'd soon have.

After a few minutes, those aboard the *Daphne* noticed something unusual about the ship heading toward them. It was traveling faster than any boat of that time could sail. As the strange vessel drew closer, the men began firing warning shots. When those did no good, the *Daphne's* captain ordered his crew to fire directly at the other vessel. But the shots had no effect. The strange ship continued to approach theirs at top speed. Seconds later, the threatening vision cut right across the *Daphne's* bow.

Then it vanished.

It's said that at exactly the moment that apparition crossed the *Daphne's* bow, her crew swam into the sunken cave where the treasures lay. Not one of those sailors ever returned to the surface again. The ship's captain tried to sail back to England but with half of his crew gone he wasn't able to navigate the ocean and the ship sank.

Eleven years later, on a July night in the same area of the Pacific Ocean, another ship, the *Bacchante*, was sailing on peaceful seas when its crew spotted an unknown craft in the distance. As the other ship came closer and closer, it became obvious that something was very wrong. The ocean was calm for miles and miles around, yet this other ship heaved and tossed and seemed to be fighting a dreadful storm.

In keeping with the laws of the sea, the captain of the *Bacchante* changed his ship's course to help the struggling vessel. As they came closer to the strange craft, the sailors realized this was not a normal ship. This vessel only existed in a cloud of fog or mist. It was a phantom ship. The *Bacchante's* captain did everything he could to get away from the evil illusion, but it was too late. The same curse that befell the *Daphne* had already taken hold of his ship.

By morning, several of the sailors aboard the *Bacchante* had died from bizarre accidents. Another ship passing by stopped to help the terrified sailors remaining on the cursed *Bacchante*. But even though the rescuers took the remaining sailors on board their own ship, the *Bacchante's* entire crew was dead within the month.

Worse, the stories of that phantom ship don't end there. The eerie manifestation was seen five times between 1893 and 1911, and there have been several similar reports since then from locations all over the South Pacific.

Do these evil apparitions really still sail the seas or does the powerful and lonely sea sharpen the sailors' senses to the point that they are somehow able to see into the past?

We'll never know.

The Terrifying Titanic

On April 10, 1912, the huge and luxurious ship *Titanic* set sail from England on its first and only voyage across the Atlantic Ocean. The *Titanic's* owners were so sure that their beautiful new ship would be a success that they had already started to build another just like her. They called these two magnificent ships "floating palaces" and declared that sailing across the Atlantic would never be the same again. On their ships, the voyage would be a long, elegant party for anyone rich enough to afford to travel first-class.

The *Titanic's* owners assured the passengers that the luxury liner was not only grand but also, absolutely safe. "The ship is unsinkable," they are said to have claimed. Wealthy people from all over the world could hardly wait to buy their expensive tickets to sail away on the grand ship's first—and last—sailing.

We all know that the voyage ended in tragedy of mammoth proportions. On April 14, 1912, the ship's crew was either not paying attention or not reporting what they saw, because the grand vessel hit a floating mountain of ice and sank in the frigid water, taking 1522 souls to the bottom of the North Atlantic.

Other stories about the ship are less well known.

Fourteen years before the *Titanic* left port, a man named Morgan Robertson had a vivid and detailed nightmare. In his terrible dream, a huge and luxurious ship, filled with wealthy passengers, sank in freezing water during the month of April. The name of the ship in Robertson's nightmare was the *Titan*. The dream was so clear that he wrote down every detail of it and later published the story as a book.

Early in 1912, as soon as Robertson heard about the magnificent new ship the *Titanic*, he realized that it was almost identical, even in name, to the one he'd dreamed and written about. Robertson thought of warning the *Titanic's* owners about the scary similarities between the real ship and his dream ship, but he was afraid that people would think he was crazy. So he did nothing.

Maybe he was correct and the *Titanic's* owners would have laughed at him for comparing their wonderful new ship to a mere bad dream. Would the company have taken his premonition seriously? Tragically, we can never know but we do know that people didn't learn from the tragedy of the *Titanic* because in another strange twist, in 1930, less than twenty years after the *Titanic* sank, a British company announced that it was building an enormous and luxurious air ship called a dirigible, or blimp. They named the craft simply *R101* but bragged that is was like the *Titanic*. They called it the *Titanic* of the air.

You've likely seen modern-day blimps on television during sporting events like football games. These air ships are big, oblong balloons, each with a large basket hanging beneath it. They often have advertisements for tires painted on their sides and they show viewers what the sports field looks like from high above. Today's blimps hold very few people, but in 1930, the basket underneath the mammoth *R101* was more like a small hotel, big enough to transport dozens of people.

By comparing the *R101* to the doomed ship *Titanic*, the owners of the aircraft were trying to tell people that the blimp would be the most luxurious way for rich people to travel. Just as the *Titanic's* builders had, the owners of the *R101* had complete confidence in their craft's safety. They advertised it as being "as safe as a house."

Like the *Titanic*, the *R101* crashed on its first ever journey, mostly as a result of the crew not paying enough attention. Like Robertson's dream of the *Titanic*, this tragedy was also foretold. In 1926, a psychic named Eileen Garrett had a vision of the deadly crash of a dirigible, before the *R101* had even been built.

At the time, Garrett didn't report her precognition because no one knew that such a craft would ever be built. Two years later, though, Garrett had a second psychic sighting about the deadly accident and contacted Sir Sefton Brancker, the government official responsible for the project. The man ignored her warning and had workers carry on building the airship. In 1929, Garrett had a third psychic sighting of the blimp. This time she saw it engulfed in flames and falling from the sky. Perhaps because no one had paid any attention to her previous message, Eileen Garrett did not tell anyone of her third vision.

On 5, October 1930, her predictions came true. The *R101* crashed in France, killing almost everyone aboard.

A few days after the deadly accident, Garrett conducted a séance to communicate with the spirits of those who'd died in the crash. The ghost of the *R101*'s captain spoke through her and gave details about the blimp and its crash that only its captain would know. Newspapers all over the world carried the story of Eileen Garrett's psychic abilities.

In all, the psychic held seven séances to find out all she could about R101's tragic failure. Several of those killed in the crash, including Sir Sefton Brancker, the man who disregarded Garrett's warnings about the *R101*, came back in spirit form to explain that the crash had been caused by a gas leak, which had sparked a fire. The psychic's vision of flames shooting from the blimp had been a hundred percent accurate.

Clearly it would be wise to turn down any invitation to travel on any vehicle ever compared to either the *Titanic*.

Those warnings from the other side were eerily and deadly accurate.

Spectral Air Show

On a clear night when the moon is full and bright, if you happen to be near Biggin Hill in England's county of Kent, be sure to look up to the heavens. You just might be treated to a spectacular air show because some nights, a squadron of Spitfires, the famous British fighter planes, can be seen and heard flying across the skies. Perhaps you think that would be a perfectly normal sight and sound. After all, airplanes are built to do just that—fly in the sky.

But these planes are from World War II.

What makes the squadron's appearance even spookier is that often, the day after the eerily mysterious planes have droned about the sky, the people who live near Biggin Hill will notice strangers in town. These strangers are dressed in identical trench coats and they stop local residents on the streets to ask for directions to different spots in town. But just as the people are about to reply, the well-dressed strangers disappear in a way that no flesh-and-blood person could.

Neither mystery—the World War II Spitfires flying

more than sixty years after they were retired, or the well dressed, vanishing visitors—has ever been solved. Most folks simply believe that both the old airplanes and the strangers are ghostly echoes from the terrible days of the war. Perhaps, for these pilots and their planes, the war has never ended.

His Last Mission

Fighter pilots need equal amounts of skill and courage and this was never more true than during World War I. The best of those brave pilots were called "aces" and their heroics were acknowledged and admired by all. Stories of their exploits lived longer than the pilots themselves did.

Back in the day, a man named Bert was one of the finest fighter pilots who ever flew a mission. He shot down twenty-eight enemy planes and was shot down three times himself. The last time he crashed and burned, Bert hid in a shell-hole without food or water for two days before he managed to get to safety.

Once the war ended Bert became a test pilot, but soon rheumatism that began in the shell-hole became so painful that he had to give up flying entirely. After that he rarely left his easy chair.

When World War II broke out, Bert ached to get back into the cockpit. As a matter of fact, his dying words were,

"I'd give anything if I could have one more smack at the enemy."

A few hours after Bert spoke those words, enemy planes flew over his hometown. Most of his neighbours ran for cover but a few people peeked out their windows when they heard the roar of a particular plane's engine. When they did, they saw a World War I biplane storming through the middle of the German planes.

Some folks thought the pilot must have been a collector of vintage aircraft but the old biplane carried the Royal Air Force markings. The plane flew so low that people could see the pilot in the open cockpit. Even with his flight goggles covering his eyes there were still those who recognized Bert.

With the skill and courage he was known for, Bert flew straight at a pair of enemy bombers. The planes veered and crashed into one another, blowing both of them to bits. A third plane, trying to avoid the mid-air collision nosedived into a field.

Later, an observer said, "I couldn't believe my eyes, that old biplane knocked three planes out of the air at once."

When it was all over, the neighbours scrambled to find out who had managed to get hold of a vintage biplane. It was definitely a single-seat fighter from the last war, they said, although it seemed to be flying incredibly fast.

In the chaos of the crashes no one saw the old plane fly away and it was never traced.

Bert's body was found later that day. It seemed he'd died with a smile on his face.

John Lennon's Old Haunt

Near Central Park in New York City, stands a big, old apartment building called the Dakota. Some people think the building is so ugly that they call it the "Dracula." Others think it looks elegant and they'd love to live there but almost everyone agrees that, ugly or elegant, the apartment block is very haunted.

The name of the building might be familiar to you if you know that the famous Beatle, John Lennon, lived there until December 8, 1980, when he was shot to death as he returned home. It is said that in the case of a sudden death such as Lennon's, a person's soul may stay on our earthly plane because his life's work isn't finished. Such is apparently the case with Lennon because his ghost has been seen sitting at the piano in his old apartment on the seventh floor. Perhaps he is writing even more heavenly music now than he did when he was alive.

Psychics have also seen Lennon's apparition outside the apartment building, often near the door where he was murdered. Occasionally, his ghost will flash the peace sign at those who've seen his ghostly image.

But John Lennon is not the only specter in the Dakota. When he was alive, Lennon himself even encountered one of the building's ghosts. One day, late in the 1970s, as the musician stepped into the hall outside his suite, he suddenly felt that something was somehow different. Then he thought he saw a movement in the empty corridor. As he stood quietly, trying to figure out what was happening, Lennon said he heard the sounds of disembodied weeping. This sad ghost is well known to people at the Dakota.

Another hallway ghost is the remarkably detailed image of a little girl. She has long blonde hair and wears an old-fashioned dress, white stockings and black patent-leather shoes with silver buckles on them. This spectral visitor is always seen bouncing a ball as she skips happily along the corridor, announcing in a singsong voice that today is her birthday. Although she's a happy soul, people dread seeing her. It's said that she only appears just before a death occurs in the building.

A couple we'll call the Wilsons live on the third floor of the Dakota. Both Mr. and Mrs. Wilson occasionally heard phantom footsteps walking through their apartment. Not only were the sounds unnerving but the couple knew that after a visit from the ghostly walker, one or other of them would have a bizarre accident. For example, chairs have moved as one or the other of them were about to sit down and small rugs have been yanked out from under their feet. The Wilsons wonder if the ghostly prankster once lived in their apartment.

One evening, as Mr. Wilson walked home along the sidewalk, he glanced up toward the windows of his apartment. Much to his surprise, he saw a large chandelier burning brightly in his dining room and it didn't look anything like the light fixture that the Wilsons had in their dining room! Mr. Wilson rushed to his apartment thinking that his wife had bought a new dining room light. But she hadn't. The fixture that the Wilsons had installed years ago was still there. And, it wasn't turned on.

That night, Mr. Wilson was still upset about the fancy chandelier he'd seen from the sidewalk and he decided to do some investigating. He pushed the dining room table aside and climbed up on a stepladder until he could easily see tiny details in the ceiling. There, under many coats of paint, was the outline of a bracket. The kind used to hang a big, heavy chandelier such as the one he had seen from the street just a few minutes before. Perhaps he'd seen the ghost of the former tenant's light fixture!

In another apartment in the Dakota, painters who were redecorating were constantly bothered by invisible entities. After a while they figured out that when the room began to smell musty and stale, they were about to have an unearthly visitor because that strange odour always meant that the ghost of a little boy, dressed in old-fashioned clothing, was about to appear. The apparition would watch the men for a while and then drift away, becoming less visible with each step he took back to the world beyond.

Those ghostly visits didn't bother the workers. They actually looked forward to the boy's appearances, that is, until he reappeared as a grown-up, but still with a childish face. That strange sighting disturbed all of the workers and made them eager to get away from the haunted apartment. One worker didn't get out of the suite quite soon enough. As he climbed a ladder to finish painting a spot on the ceiling, the apartment door slammed closed. Seconds, later, all the lights went out. He was alone in the dark. And up a ladder. Then something invisible grabbed the man's arm. Clearly, the phantom had lost patience with the renovations and wanted the workers out of his haunt. The man scampered down from the ladder, gathered up his gear and left in a hurry! Not surprisingly, the ghost's hijinks earned it the privacy that it was after, because not one of the workers ever entered that suite again. The new tenants who moved in apparently never complained about ghostly disturbances. Presumably the ghost didn't hold them responsible for the renovations.

Two other spirits who haunt the Dakota are the ghosts of a man called "Joe" and a young woman carrying a flower. They are less frightening—except for the shock people get when they realize that they've just seen a ghost.

Although no one can identify all of the entities at the

Dakota, the ghost in the basement is recognized every time he appears. He is the spirit of a short, bearded man with a big nose and round glasses. He's always dressed in a coat and top hat, the latest style in the 1800s. Immediately after the phantom appears, he removes his top hat with one hand and with the other hand takes off the wig he's wearing under the hat. If that's not strange enough, the odd little ghost has been known to violently shake his wig at whoever has the misfortune to have seen his image. This supernatural presence is always recognized as Edward Clark, the man who built the Dakota apartment block. He died in 1832. Perhaps his soul stayed behind to scare the people who think his building is ugly and call it the Dracula!

The Dance of the Dead

One chilly September evening, along a country road on the small Irish island of Inishark, a young woman named Colleen trudged wearily home from the village. She'd worked hard all day helping a friend who wasn't feeling well and by now she was bone tired herself. Even though she knew her brother Liam was waiting for her, Colleen had to rest for just a while. She wouldn't take long because she knew this was no time to be out by herself. After all, the hour of the dead was fast approaching.

Colleen drew her thin coat around her but the worn fabric was no match for the cold night air. She closed her eyes and imagined herself safely at home in front of the hearth. The thought warmed her soul and she might have fallen into a deep sleep right there and then if the sound of footsteps coming toward her hadn't disturbed her.

Frightened, Colleen looked up to see the pale image of a young man standing beside her. Where could he have come from? She'd been alone on the path only minutes before. Panic rose through her veins paralyzing every muscle.

"It's all right," the image told her. His voice and face were sad but kindly.

"I know you." Colleen nodded. "You're young Bram who drowned in the pond last year. How can you be here?"

"I've come because I saw that you needed me," he said and then pointed to the edge of a nearby slope.

Colleen turned her head and saw a cluster of people dressed in white. They were dancing and twirling more gracefully than she'd ever seen people move.

"Listen," the young man said cupping his hand to his ear. Colleen heard music so beautiful that it had to be otherworldly. She gazed at the dancers and longed to be one of the people. They were all islanders who had died. Their faces were as white as the filmy white clothes they wore. They were clearly enchanted by the music and didn't notice Colleen at all. Then the music stopped.

They turned their pale faces toward the frightened girl and beckoned to her with their fleshless hands.

"Run!" Bram's ghost yelled to her. "If you join the dancers you'll never be able to leave." Terrified, Colleen turned to run but the unearthly music began again, luring her toward the dancers who stared at her with empty eye sockets. Slowly Bram moved away from her and joined the group as it circled around her. Faster and faster the dancers spun until all Colleen could see was a blur of white surrounding her. Seconds later she fell to the ground in a faint.

The next thing Colleen knew she was safely at home in her bed with her brother sitting across the room. He'd found her unconscious at the side of the path and had carried her home. She told him about Bram and the dancers but he was sure she was hallucinating.

That night, as the full moon rose, Colleen lay with her eyes open and pointed to the window. "Do you hear that?" she asked Liam. He shook his head.

"Look outside," she urged.

He went to the window but all he saw was moonlight on the fields. A second later he looked back toward Colleen's bed. He could see that she had died. Grief-stricken he shook his fists toward heaven and that's when he heard the lilting music his sister had spoken of. Wrenched with the agony of losing his sister, he searched the night sky.

And that's when he saw her. His beloved sister had become one of the dancers.

To his dying day Liam said that he was sure that he saw Colleen pause just for a moment and stare back at him before she danced off with the others to the great beyond.

Lesson Learned

For 12-year-old Andrea, the worst part of living with a ghost was that she knew she had caused the haunting with her own thoughtless actions. The second worst part was that she had to keep everything a secret.

Andrea had always lived happily with her parents in their perfectly ordinary, ghost-free, house. Then one fateful summer evening, the girl did something very foolish and that night her carefree life vanished. Fear replaced happiness.

The trouble began innocently enough when Andrea and two girlfriends decided to take a shortcut through the local cemetery. If the girls had just kept walking, it's unlikely that anything bad would have occurred, but as sometimes happens, one thing led to another. For a joke, Andrea gave the friend walking next to her a bit of a shove—just hard enough to put the girl off balance. While she was trying to steady herself, that girl bumped into the third girl, who had been walking nearest to the graves.

"Cut it out!" the third girl yelled as she steadied herself. "You nearly pushed me on top of that grave."

Andrea must have been in a devilish mood because she laughed at her friend and teased, "Scared of the dead, are you?" With that, Andrea and her friends began chasing one another around the cemetery.

As they ran, the three youngsters became less and less careful about where they ran. Soon they were scurrying across graves, jumping over small headstones and hiding behind larger ones. Eventually they tired of their game and that was fortunate. After all, they knew better. They knew they were being very disrespectful to the souls of the people buried there.

That night, hours after she'd gone to bed, Andrea awoke from a deep sleep. At first she wondered what had wakened her. Everything was quiet. Nothing seemed to be wrong. That is, not until her eyes adjusted to the darkness. Then Andrea could see the image of an old man sitting in a chair across the room.

She gasped and buried her face under the covers. A moment later, as the comfort and warmth of the blankets began to lull Andrea back to sleep, she decided that she hadn't really seen an image at all; that she'd only dreamt it.

But the next morning, that old man was still sitting in the chair across the room from Andrea's bed. Is he real? Andrea wondered. She rubbed her eyes, blinked several times and shook her head to try to make the image disappear. It didn't work. The strange man just sat there. He didn't move, he didn't even say anything. He just sat there so still that Andrea thought she was imagining him.

She grabbed her robe from the foot of her bed and put it on before getting out of bed.

Once she was out of her bedroom, the girl felt much more confident. *Wow, what a realistic dream I had,* she thought with a sigh as she wandered into the kitchen to get a bowl of cereal.

Then Andrea saw the man again. He still didn't say anything but nonetheless managed to terrify the girl by floating around the house behind her. That's what finally made her realize that, even though she couldn't see through him, her bizarre visitor must be a ghost.

For a moment, Andrea stood holding her cereal bowl in front of her and staring at the apparition. She tried to be calm but her heart raced. Then the image beside her dissolved into nothingness.

That morning at school, Andrea made a point of asking her two girlfriends if everything was well in their lives. Both girls nodded and turned the question around to Andrea who told them she was fine except maybe for having a bit of a guilty conscience about having been running all over those people's graves in the cemetery. Before her friends could respond, the school bell rang and the friends didn't see each other for the rest of the day.

At dinner, Andrea was sure that she saw the ghost floating through the dining room as the family ate dinner. She didn't say anything about it to her parents, though. After all, she could hardly tell them, "I think that our house is haunted by a ghost whose grave I disturbed while I was acting like a jerk with my friends."

Later in the evening, Andrea's father asked her to make a pot of tea. When she lifted the steaming kettle from the stove to pour the water into the teapot, she felt something twist her arm. The boiling water very nearly spilled. As she took a deep breath and steadied her hand, Andrea was sure she saw a human-shaped form, wearing an old-fashioned dress, disappearing out of the kitchen. Now she knew there were at least two ghosts in her house. The girl wondered how much more of this she was going to be able to bear.

What was going to be more difficult, she wondered, living with ghosts following her around or telling her parents what she had done? After making the tea, she watched the slightly transparent apparition of an old woman join the old man's spirit in the hallway. Then Andrea realized that she would have to gather her courage and tell her parents that their house was haunted. Worse, she would have to admit that there was no mystery about the ghosts. She had caused the problem with her own foolishness.

But before Andrea had a chance to explain the situation to her parents, the haunting became worse. The family was quietly watching television when Andrea suddenly started to speak in a strange voice. She announced to her parents that she was the daughter of a French doctor and that she had been born in 1851. Needless to say, the strange voice and words coming out of Andrea's mouth terrified her parents. They rushed her to the hospital, but none of the doctors could find anything wrong. By then the voice was quiet and Andrea was just as bewildered as everyone else about the uncontrollable words that she had spoken.

It's possible that the disturbed spirits enjoyed all the trouble they were causing because by noon the next day, they were appearing to Andrea's mother as well. The man's image even reached out to hit the woman but his ghostly hand went right through her body as if she wasn't even there.

That was more than enough for Andrea's family. They had no desire to live in a haunted house and so that very afternoon they made plans to move.

Six months later, when Andrea was visiting her friends in the old neighbourhood, she happened to walk past her old house. It was clear that no one lived there. Something about the place drew Andrea to it. Slowly, she walked toward the house and around to the back door. Oddly, the door was open. The girl walked into the back hall.

Instantly, she shivered from an unnatural cold that surrounded her. Then she felt two invisible hands wrapping themselves around her neck. Choking badly, she tried to get away. Then, seconds later, the phantom hands released the girl and pushed her back out the door into the warmth and fresh air.

Andrea never told her parents about her last encounter with the ghosts.

She also never again showed any kind of foolish disrespect to those who had already passed on to the afterlife.

Ski Spirits

"Come in, come in, come in," the man fussed as he opened the door to the mountain chalet. "Don't let all the heat get out through the door. It's freezing out there, but the fire's been going steady in here for a while and you'll warm up in not time."

Kip muttered his thanks, stood his skis up against a spot near the door and walked into the warm log cabin.

"I'm grateful that you're here in this cabin," he told the older man. "I very nearly got caught in that avalanche a moment ago. You must have heard it, did you?"

"I did hear it. This is avalanche country, for sure. My name's Don, Don Bennett, and I live here. I just love it. It's my little piece of heaven."

"Hi, Don, nice to meet you. I'm Kip. I'm up here with a school group. I guess I shouldn't have skied away from the others but I got distracted and lost track of them. I'm sure glad you're here. I'll need some help finding my way back to the lodge," Kip told the man who smiled slightly and nodded toward a pair of chairs by the fireplace.

The two chatted for a while, mostly about skiing: its dangers and its pleasures. Their conversation wound down naturally and Don stood up. "You get some rest now, Kip. I'll bring in some more firewood."

"Sure you don't want any help?" Kip asked, inwardly hoping that he could just sit where he was in front of the roaring fire. When the man didn't answer, the tired skier opened the door and looked outside. But Don was nowhere to be seen.

That's when Kip noticed that there weren't any tracks in the snow, not even the ones he had made a few minutes earlier.

What the heck's going on here?

On the verge of panic, Kip closed the door. The cabin was cozy and had everything a mountain ski chalet should have. There was just one big room. The log walls smelled of cedar and the rafters were open. Snow shoes and animal pelts hung from the walls. A big dining room table took up most of the space but there was still room for a bed in one corner and, of course, the two over-stuffed easy chairs in front of the fireplace.

An old newspaper lay open on the dining room table and, not knowing what else to do, Kip sat down and began to scan the pages. A small article toward the bottom of the page caught his eye.

The headline read;

Another Skier Lost in Avalanche
Don Bennett, a dentist with a large city practice, is missing and presumed dead after an avalanche swept through the valley where he had been skiing. Experienced searchers working through the daylight hours yesterday found no trace of the man's body. The search has now been called off.

Dr. Bennett leaves a wife and three grown children. "At least he died doing what he loved," commented the man's oldest daughter.

Dead? Why did the newspaper report that Don was dead? Kip wondered. *He isn't dead. I just talked to him. He's as alive as I am.*

A few seconds later, the young skier slowly began to understand. He had it backwards. Don wasn't as alive as Kip was. Kip was as dead as Don was. That avalanche hadn't missed him after all. The newly created ghost smiled. Don hadn't been kidding when he'd said that this chalet was his little piece of heaven! And now, it was Kip's; at least until there was another knock on the door. *Better get that fire built up,* Kip thought, as he began to settle into his afterlife.

A Small Visitor

Jennifer's dollhouse stood in the corner of her bedroom. Even though she hadn't played with it for years and it looked a little out of place by now, the teenager still enjoyed having it in her room. She smiled when she looked at the miniature house and remembered all the happy hours she'd spent arranging the furniture and moving the tiny dolls from one room to another, always pretending the small plastic figures were real people.

One hot spring day, long after Jennifer had outgrown the toy, she hurried into her bedroom to change into her tennis clothes. Her mind was on getting to the tennis courts quickly, because she and her best friend Tracy had arranged a game of doubles against two of their classmates. If the other girls were as good at the game as they'd been bragging they were, then this was going to be a challenge.

But the moment Jennifer stepped into her bedroom, thoughts of friends and tennis flew from her mind. She could hardly believe her eyes. There, kneeling in front of her dollhouse, was a little girl about four years old. The child was dressed in a long, dark skirt with an apron over top of it and a blouse so white that it almost glowed. She had brown braids wrapped around her head.

She looks like pictures I've seen of children who lived a hundred years ago, Jennifer thought in amazement.

Fascinated by the strange image, Jennifer could only stand and stare. The little soul was leaning forward just a bit and happily playing with Jen's beloved dollhouse. The child didn't seem to be aware of anything around her. She was having too much fun playing, in exactly the way Jennifer herself had years before.

Suddenly, perhaps sensing the teenager's presence, the little wraith turned her head toward Jennifer and the two girls stared at one another across the room and across time. Jennifer knew instantly that she was glancing into the world of the supernatural because although the child was as clear as she could be, Jen could see right through her. There could be no question about it; this was a ghost, the ghost of a little girl was playing with Jennifer's dollhouse.

At first, the two gazed at each another in wonder but then the child's image began to fade. It seemed to Jennifer as though the entity had been made from thousands of tiny points of light. The bright speckles twinkled before fading away. Soon the entire image disappeared.

Nothing about the spirit child frightened Jennifer but it took her a minute to get used to the fact that she'd actually seen a ghost. Slowly, Jennifer walked to her bed and sat down to think about the amazing experience she'd just had. By then her friends and the tennis game were far, far from her mind.

After that, whenever Jennifer saw her old dollhouse, she smiled about more than just her childhood memories because it made her happy to know that another child, a child who must have lived long ago, had also enjoyed playing with that dollhouse.

Jennifer's grown up now and moved into her own home. She still has her old dollhouse but the little ghost has never visited again.

Castle Ghosts

Not many people live in castles these days, but years ago many wealthy families did just that. Judging by the number of ghosts in the castles that are still standing, those early owners must have been so fond of their homes that they wanted to stay there forever—even after the castle walls had tumbled down.

Berry Pomeroy Castle, in the south of England, is an example of just such a haunted castle. Today the place is nothing more than a crumbling pile of ruins atop a wind-swept hill but even so it's still a popular tourist attraction, in large part due to its ghosts. The story of how that castle came to be haunted is an interesting one.

Centuries ago, the lady of the castle took sick and her husband called the doctor to come at once. After the doctor had seen the patient he noticed a beautiful young woman standing on a staircase. He was surprised and later he told a maid about the lovely girl he had seen. The servant became hysterical. When she finally calmed down, the young woman explained to the doctor that the "person" on the stairs wasn't a person at all. It was one of the castle's ghosts, a ghost that no one ever wanted to see because this was a crisis apparition; a ghost who only appeared before a tragedy was about to strike. The maid was afraid that the lady of the house was going to die but the doctor assured her that her employer was already getting better and would be well again in a few days.

A week later, both the doctor and the maid were proven to be correct. The lady of the house had recovered, but the maid was dead.

Legend has it that the castle's harbinger of death is the spirit of a woman who once lived in the castle. She was a cruel person and, it is thought that as punishment for her cruelty, her spirit was doomed to appear at times of impending death.

Fortunately, no one has seen that image for years but even today, if you dare to get close to the remains of the castle, you might meet the spirit of Margaret de Pomeroy who haunts the castle dungeon. In life, Margaret was an extraordinarily pretty young woman. Her older sister, Eleanor wasn't nearly as beautiful.

It was their misfortune to both fall in love with the same man. The sisters argued endlessly about who would marry the man. One day, after a particularly nasty quarrel, Eleanor locked Margaret into the dungeon and left her there until she starved to death.

People who have seen Margaret's ghost report that she is still very beautiful, but they also note that she is as dangerous as she is attractive. The castle's current caretakers warn visitors that, "On certain nights of the year, the lovely Margaret is said to arise from her entombed dungeon, walk along the castle's ramparts and beckon the beholder to come join her in the dungeon below."

In addition, at least three other ghosts can be seen at Berry Pomeroy Castle. The Blue Lady wanders about the ruins wearing a blue hooded cape. It is said that she is looking for her baby, who died soon after birth. There are also the spirits of a young man and a woman who fell in love, but their families forbade them from being together. In death, the couple is seen forever reaching out to one another, but never quite managing to touch.

It would seem that a visit to Berry Pomeroy Castle is a must for anyone who loves haunted history!

The Haunted Bridge

Long ago, during the early 1800s in Vermont, there lived a beautiful young woman named Emily. Her parents guarded their daughter very carefully but it wasn't because they were afraid she would be harmed. No, the selfish old couple wanted to make sure their beautiful child was kept safe so that she would grow up to marry a rich man who would support them in their old age.

When she was a little girl, Emily accepted her parents' plan but, as she grew older, the girl began to think for herself. She came to resent being told who to marry, especially since her parents were lazy and didn't want to work hard themselves.

One day, when Emily was in town running errands for her parents, she met a handsome young man. It was love at first sight. The love-struck couple talked for hours that day and made arrangements to meet again that night. "Meet me near the covered bridge at midnight," the man told Emily. "I'll be there with my horse and we'll ride off together until we come to a town where no one knows us. Once we're there, we'll marry and live happily ever after."

"I'll be there," Emily answered joyfully, sure that all her wishes were about to come true.

That night, just before midnight, Emily slipped out of her parents' home, as quiet as a mouse so as not to waken them. She fled to the bridge where she was to meet her beloved, but he was not there. She waited and waited, but he did not arrive.

As darkness turned to dawn, Emily finally realized that the man was never going to come to carry her away to another town. The girl's heart was broken. If she went home, her parents would punish her horribly for having left the house without their permission. She would survive the punishment she was sure, but only because they needed their daughter to ensure their own future. Emily could see no hope of happiness for herself. The man she loved had played her for a fool and her parents only wanted to use her.

Slowly the poor girl undid the sash on her dress, climbed to the roof of the bridge and hanged herself.

By now no one remembers who found Emily's body or who informed her parents that they had lost their ticket to an easy life. Very little else is known about this sad love story except that since then, people have reported seeing a filmy image resembling a young woman walking through the covered bridge. She is dressed in an old-fashioned frock tied with a sash. They say the image simply vanishes when witnesses approach her.

Young couples driving home around midnight have reported hearing rubbing sounds on the roof of their car as they drive through the bridge. Local rumour has it that Emily's ghostly feet still dangle from the rafters and brush along the cars roofs.

Photographs taken near the bridge often show strange circles of light. People who study the world of the supernatural say that these "orbs," as they have come to be known, are manifestations of the spirits that haunt a place. Other people report feeling small pockets of extremely cold air floating throughout the bridge, even on the warmest summer days. More than one psychic who visited the old wooden structure reported experiencing extreme neck pain, as though she was being strangled. Still others are sure the air pressure inside the bridge is very different than it is outside the bridge.

But the most intriguing story about the bridge came from a man named Greg. He will never forget his experience on that bridge on a fall day in 1990.

Greg was with his girlfriend. He wouldn't reveal her name so we'll refer to her as Noreen. She came from a wealthy and proud family in England. Greg and Noreen had been touring the eastern United States and Canada. He had planned to ask her to marry him before they headed home.

Greg had enjoyed their trip. He'd been delighted by the

beautiful fall colors and picturesque settings they'd seen, but Noreen was bored and unappreciative, particularly so when they saw an old covered bridge a few miles from Stowe, Vermont.

Greg recalled, "I was interested in getting some photos and so I clambered out of the car and onto the old bridge. Noreen meanwhile, stared at her reflection in the car's rear view mirror. She told me to be quick and that in England there were much older and more interesting bridges than this."

Trying to ignore his girlfriend's unpleasant comments, Greg walked toward the bridge. That was when, for the first and only time in his life, the man's reality began to shift. As he approached the bridge, which is less than fifty feet long, it suddenly seemed to be much longer, almost endless and his automatic camera, which was normally very reliable, simply refused to focus.

Despite these strange events, the man kept walking into the covered bridge. As his eyes adjusted to the dark interior, he realized he was not alone. There, in front of him, stood a young woman.

"She had a very small waist and blond, shoulder-length hair that curled in ringlets around her face. She stood in a shaft of dusty sunlight, staring into the distance, as if waiting for someone. She wore an old-style white dress that extended from her laced-up shoes all the way to her neck.

She seemed aware of me," Greg recalled, "and unconcerned by my presence."

Not wanting to be impolite, Greg said "hello," but received no reply. He turned his attention back to his camera that still would not focus properly. "My camera was hopelessly messed up and I felt very strange. I asked if she was waiting for someone. She didn't reply but turned her head toward me. She had beautiful green eyes and a porcelain-doll beauty to her."

Finally the entity smiled at Greg before admitting that, she was waiting for someone. She said she'd been "waiting for a long, long time."

Greg explained to her that his intended fiancée was just outside the bridge waiting in the car and he offered to drive the waiting woman into town. The image replied, "I don't think your girlfriend would like that." Then he began to walk back to the car. The apparition called out to him, warning that marrying Noreen would be a mistake.

Upon hearing those words, Greg swung around instantly but the delicate vision was gone. He turned back and continued to walk toward the car. As he came closer, Greg could see by her expression that Noreen was angry at having been kept waiting. The two drove away in silence each concentrating on their own thoughts.

Months later, an English teacher with a solid reputation told Greg the ghostly legend of a girl named Emily who haunted a covered bridge in Stowe, Vermont. He was shocked because he knew for certain that he had met that very ghost. Not only had he met here but he had followed her advice by not marrying Noreen. And he had never regretted following Emily's ghostly advice.

Evil Lives Here

The "thing" that had haunted the old house for years was evil. The story of why the house was haunted had been forgotten long ago. All that anyone remembered was that the building had been moved from town onto Ken's family's land and that it had always been home to a nasty spirit.

One day when Ken was away, his wife, Dawn went out into the back yard for some fresh air. As she did, the door behind her slammed closed, locking her out of the house. She had no choice but to wait outside until Ken came home from work. Those hours gave her lots of time to think and wonder about living in a haunted house. Perhaps that is exactly what the ghost intended for her to do, to think, to wonder and to be afraid.

Not long after that episode, the couple had friends over for a card game. That evening, they all heard heavy footsteps tramping across the floor of an upstairs room. Thinking that someone had broken in, Ken ran up the stairs, ready to tackle the intruder. As soon as his foot hit the top stair, he realized that the sounds had come from a room that was used as a storeroom. No one could walk across that floor because it was covered with boxes, wall-to-wall and floor to ceiling. Apparently Ken and Dawn's friends weren't keen on playing cards while an active ghost walked above their heads because they didn't waste any time in saying their good-byes!

When Dawn first brought her cat, Tiger, to the old house, that poor animal had no peace. The cat would run from room to room as though fleeing from some terrible terror. Sometimes, when he had been sleeping peacefully, Tiger would suddenly jump to his feet. Then, with his fur standing straight out from his body, the cat would stare at something that was completely invisible to human eyes.

Like most ghosts, this entity was drawn to electric lights and light switches. As a result, Ken and Dawn rarely got a good night's sleep. Most nights, Ken had to get up at least once to turn off the light in their bedroom closet. What set his nerves on edge more than the disturbed sleep was that the phantom knew exactly which light would shine directly at his eyes as he slept.

Dawn once watched in horror as a lamp suddenly slid across the living room. Impossibly, the lamp actually gained speed as it moved and stopped only when it had smashed against the wall and broken into tiny pieces.

One day when he was alone in the house, Ken was sure he heard someone fall from the top of the staircase to the bottom. He realized his patience for the nasty presence was nearly at an end when he shouted into the "empty" house, "I hope you hurt yourself!" The hauntings were clearly taking a toll on the man's kind nature. "It was like living in a horror novel," he explained.

Ken and Dawn continued living in the awful old house until their son Jay was born. By the time Jay was just a toddler he sensed that certain parts of the house were not safe. "It's coming for me!" the child would shriek. When his parents asked him what was coming for him, he shivered with fear and whispered, "It looks like poop."

In the spring of that year, the couple began to build a new house on the same large property. By summer the little family had happily moved into their new home.

Their escape from the haunted house was an enormous relief, even though they did wonder what they should do about the dreadful old house that still stood nearby. Ken hesitated to tear it down for fear of angering whatever presence still resided there. In the end, they decided just to ignore the place and leave it to rot, as any normal structure would do. Unfortunately, that house was not normal, it was paranormal and, now that the family had moved out, the evil thing could do as it pleased. And it did.

At night, Ken and Dawn frequently saw lights shining in the abandoned house even though there was no electricity hooked up. During daylight, they could hear the sounds of hammering and sawing coming from it. Neither of them investigated the noises.

Every once in a while, though, they had to enter the horrible old place. The first day Ken went back in, it was warm and sunny outside. Inside, it was ice-cold, clammy and dark. Ken desperately wanted to be back outside before the spirit knew he'd been in. But he failed. As soon as he set foot inside, he heard a heartbreaking noise coming from the basement. It sounded like newborn puppies crying for their mother. Ken knew that there couldn't be any puppies in the house. Those mournful sounds were the cruel phantom's way of luring him into the basement. He fled to safety as fast as his shaking legs would carry him. No one ever found any trace of any puppies in that basement. All that has ever been found is the occasional body of a field mouse or a squirrel that had died in the abandoned house. But those little corpses were creepy enough because they hadn't rotted like they should have. They were mummified.

Strangely, for many years after Dawn and Ken moved out, the old house remained as clean as the day they left it. No spider webs clung to the walls or ceilings. No tumble-weeds of dust gathered in the corners of the rooms. Even the frame of the house stayed strong, not aging or sagging as it should have. Whatever unnatural force resided there seemed to have made time stand still.

This abnormal situation went on until one very cold winter's day when Dawn saw the door of the abandoned house fly open. She watched in fear as, for just a second, a blurry gray, oddly shaped mass formed on the porch and then floated away as if a gust of wind had blown it.

"After that the situation changed," Ken explained. "The house is a more natural thing now. It's got bugs, it's rotting and there are live mice, cobwebs and dust inside."

Even so, the couple won't tear the house down for fear of disturbing any evil that might linger there. Instead, they wait for natural, not supernatural, forces to cause the house to crumble.

A Helpful Spirit

Here's an intriguing little tale about a person who was very important in life and very helpful in death.

Gouverneur Morris lived in New York State and he was one of the men responsible for drafting the Constitution of the United States. He died in 1815, leaving his young wife and an infant son. On New Year's Eve, 1816, Morris's spirit appeared to show his widow the secret spot in their house where he had hidden valuables that she could sell in order to support herself financially while she raised the child.

After that, it would seem that the man's spirit rested in peace for his image was never seen again.

The Most Haunted House in England

Borley Rectory in southeast England was a gloomy, twenty-three room red brick mansion built in 1863 for a man with a most impressive (and funny) name: Reverend Henry Dawson Ellis Bull. The good reverend needed such a big home because he and his wife had fourteen children. In addition to all the family members, their house was also home to several active ghosts. There were so many ghosts that the Borley Rectory was often called the most haunted house in England.

As soon as the Bull family moved in, they began to hear phantom footsteps as well as strange tapping noises and bells ringing where there weren't any bells. Lights shone in the windows of empty rooms. Phantom voices called out from everywhere and nowhere. Sudden cold spots and strange odours manifested mysteriously and then disappeared just as mysteriously. The glass in the windows cracked when no one was near them. Small objects disappeared. A phantom coach pulled by phantom horses frequently drove up to the rectory and once the family saw a coach driven by two headless coachmen.

One of the most intriguing entities in the place was the ghost of a nun. Her image was so solid and life-like that when Reverend Bull's daughters first saw her, they weren't at all frightened. They were sure she was a living being. It was only after the silent figure moved past them that the girls noticed the nun wasn't walking, but gliding, just above the ground. A few moments later they also realized that they had only seen the nun's habit moving, floating as if the person inside the robe was invisible. Then, as the girls continued to stare in amazement, the vision slowly dissolved before disappearing completely.

The legend of the phantom nun has its haunted tendrils entwined into the time before construction of Borley Rectory. Townsfolk generally believed that the rectory had been built on the site of a former monastery. According to local legend, in life the phantom nun was the pitiful soul who had been imprisoned into a brick wall in that monastery, when she was still alive!

When Reverend Bull died in the summer of 1928, his son took over the rectory. The old man must have been reluctant to leave his home because his ghost haunted the place for many years after his death.

Eventually the reverend's son retired and moved away from the ghost-filled mansion. For years after that, the rectory stood vacant because the ministers appointed to the

Borley Church knew the place was haunted and refused to live in it.

Finally, Reverend Lionel Foyster and his wife, Marianne agreed to move in. As soon as they did, poltergeist activity began. Keys would fly out of door locks. Horrible smells and strange noises followed the Foysters through the house. Heavy pieces of furniture slid around as though being pushed by a strong, but invisible, force.

As if all of that wasn't hard enough to live with, the poltergeist was about to get much more active. Mysterious messages were scrawled on the walls of various rooms in the rectory; all of them pleaded with Marianne to get help. It was never clear, though, who it was she was to get help for, herself or the rectory's angry spirit. Stones and rocks rained down from the ceilings of whichever room Marianne ran to. Once, when she was alone in a room, she was slapped on the face so hard that the blow left a bruise and blackened her eyes. The next terrifying attack nearly suffocated her. Finally, after five years of being tormented by paranormal attacks, the woman and her husband moved away from the haunted house.

Harry Price, then a famous psychic researcher, had heard about the unnatural events in the big old stone home. He decided to move into the rectory and investigate the haunting. Price witnessed doors banging, bells ringing, objects moving (and sometimes breaking!), all in empty rooms. He also endured sudden cold or hot spots in the house, as well as apparitions and even a ghostly choir singing beautiful, but supernatural music.

The last resident of the house was Captain W. H. Gregson. He lived there, apparently undisturbed by any paranormal forces, until midnight on February 27, 1939 when a mysterious fire broke out in the rectory. Some say the fire was started when a book flew from a shelf and knocked over a kerosene lamp.

Even the fire didn't stop the haunting though because in 1951, the phantom nun passed so close to a group of ghost hunters that they even heard her robes rustle as she glided along. Then, in 1975, a film crew saw ghost lights at the site and their tape recorder picked up "strange noises."

Two years later, on a road near the haunted site, paranormal specialist Steven Jenkins and his wife stared in horror as the images of four men suddenly appeared directly in front of their car. The apparitions were carrying a coffin. They disappeared as quickly as they had appeared. On their next visit, Mrs. Jenkins took a photograph of her husband. When the film was developed, they discovered images of faces superimposed on the trees in the background.

In 1944, the haunted rectory was finally demolished but even today, people are fascinated by the story. One investigator called it "the haunting that refused to go away," and he was correct because after the house was torn down, a little boy picked up a brick from the rubble that remained and buried it in his schoolyard. Now that school is widely rumoured to be haunted.

Life might be short but apparently, in this case anyway, the afterlife isn't!

WITCH OR WEREWOLF?

All the townsfolk in the small English village of Ashton knew about their strange and mysterious neighbour, Mrs. Prouse and frankly, she made them nervous. She was a big, heavy-set woman with long, messy hair and she had the strangest eyes anyone had ever seen; one eye was green and the other was yellow.

The villagers always wondered about the odd collections of things she kept in her house. Certainly no one else in town had a supply of bat wings, snake eyes, dried toads or bird feathers, to say nothing of the array of odd-looking containers she kept them in. One particularly curious container was a three-handled cup, the likes of which no one in those parts had ever seen before.

Many people admitted that Mrs. Prouse scared them. Others maintained that, although the old lady made them a bit jittery, she was nothing but a crazy fool and was not to be feared. Everyone agreed though, that if they were troubled; about their health, their romances, their crops or anything else that might not be right in their lives then Mrs. Prouse was the person to see. Often, after just one meeting with the old woman, their problems were gone.

Depending on the complaint, Mrs. Prouse might sing a chant as she boiled dried animal bones in a cauldron or she might stick pins into scary-looking dolls. Still other times, the weird old lady might have the person drink a dreadful-tasting tea that she had prepared from some awful-smelling powder and served in her curious three-handled cup. Whatever remedy she gave them, Mrs. Prouse's patients soon found their problems had flown away like a witch on a broomstick.

Women often sought her advice because, in spite of her age, Mrs. Prouse's skin was beautifully, almost unnaturally, smooth, as silky as a baby's. Of course, this quirk only added to the villagers' uneasiness about what powers she might actually have.

One day, though, the curious folks suddenly forgot their fascination with the strange old lady. That was the day after the first sightings of a mysterious wolf. It wasn't just the strange animal's howling that disturbed the people of Ashton, they were used to sleeping through the sounds of wolves baying at the moon. No, this noise was more troubling, louder and definitely more mournful.

After only a few nights of the eerie racket, villagers armed with rifles headed out to hunt down the eerie animal.

One of their shots struck the beast's left leg. When they last saw the wolf, it was whimpering and limping away.

When Mrs. Prouse was seen in town the next day. She was limping badly. Everyone noticed this strange coincidence and by noon the entire village was abuzz with gossip. The bravest man in town was chosen to ask the old woman why she was favouring her left leg.

"I cut myself while I was chopping wood," she replied curtly, before using her good leg to drag herself off.

When the eerie baying sounds had not been heard for a number of nights, a small group of curious folk decided to pay a visit to the dilapidated Prouse cottage. The gate to the creepy old place was rusty and screeched loudly in protest when it was opened. Weeds had grown so tall around the house that they almost blocked the front door completely.

Two people held back the tangled overgrowth while a third person pushed open the entranceway and stepped inside. The house was empty. Empty of anything alive that is. But the smell of decay always lingers and no combination of rude words could describe the terrible stench that wafted out of the dark and gloomy place.

Filled with equal parts of determination, courage, fear and fascination, the frightened trio went into the rundown old house. Just seconds later, their bravery gone, all three ran to escape. Still, no one could say exactly where the smell came from.

The next day, the three returned. This time they were

accompanied by dozens of other villagers, anyone willing to take the terrifying risk of visiting the unnatural place. The group silently approached the gate, each person dreading what he or she was about to see.

But Mrs. Prouse's house was simply not there. It had disintegrated, its timbers rotted and fallen.

"This land is cursed!" one man cried out.

"It is evil!" shouted another.

"It is haunted!" screamed a third before the villagers fled from the spooky scene.

Years later a newcomer moved onto the abandoned land where the strange old cottage once stood. While cleaning decades' worth of debris out of an over-grown well on the property, the man came across a skeleton—a very strange skeleton. Some of the bones appeared to be from a dog or a wolf. Others were human. A bullet lay imbedded in one leg bone and, lying beside the bizarre arrangement of bones, was a strange-looking cup—a cup with three handles. The man didn't touch either the cup or any of the bones but even so the sight filled him with such dread that he fled immediately and settled somewhere else.

To this day, the land on which Mrs. Prouse once lived, lies abandoned; by the living, that is and perhaps that shouldn't be too surprising. After all, wolves and witches have long been associated with one another. They are called werewolves.

Was Mrs. Prouse a witch? Was she a phantom wolf? Was

she a werewolf? Was she the ghost of a wolf that had come back in the form of a spooky old woman? Isn't it interesting that everyone else who drank out of the three-handled cup found their troubles went away. While Mrs. Prouse's troubles didn't.

Today we are unlikely to solve this paranormal puzzle, but if you ever see a three-handled cup, it would probably be best not to touch it!

The Original Angry Birds

Every year Kyle looked forward to the first weekend of summer, not just because it meant the beginning of school holidays but also because it was the one weekend in the entire year that his Uncle Dave came to visit. Dave was a world traveler and always had exciting adventures to tell. Like the time he'd been in a small European village nestled in a valley ...

"It was a strange little place, this one," Kyle's uncle began. "Many of the women in the village were old. I mean really old, over a hundred years old! That was creepy enough but the stories these old women told were even creepier. The worst one was about the ancient evil phantoms—super-natural beasts that lived in the caves and crevices of the mountains that surrounded their town."

The wrinkly, wretched-looking old crones warned that if anyone tried to climb the nearby mountain slopes, the climbers' lives would be in deadly peril. "Wicked and un-natural birds live up there," one toothless old hag confided.

Of course Dave and his friends knew that the women's tales were just legends, folklore from hundreds of years before.

"There can't be any truth to the stories," Dave told the others. "These women are so old that their minds have shrivelled. Besides, even when they were young and healthy they were simple, uneducated peasants. They wouldn't have known that there were no such things as 'spirits,' especially not the spirits of birds!"

Dave's friends nodded and one of them suggested that they should hike up the mountainside the very next day.

"Then," he explained, "when we get back to town in the evening, we can prove to these frightened people that there is nothing unnatural at all near their homes."

As he listened to his uncle a shiver of excitement ran down Kyle's spine. He wondered if Dave and his friends were more foolhardy than brave.

Early the next morning, the group of friends prepared for their trek without a worry in the world. No crazy old hags' superstitions could harm them, especially not on such a beautiful, sunny day.

At least that's what the climbers thought.

"It's good that we're here to show these simple people that there's nothing to fear," Dave told his friends confidently at the outset.

They chatted and joked among themselves as they climbed the steep slope. All went well for the better part of an hour. Then, in the blink of an eye, everything changed. The sun disappeared from view and the clear blue sky went dark. Thunderous sounds bellowed from the blackened sky. The adventurers looked toward the mountaintops. An enormous flock of huge, ugly birds circled above them. Hundreds of gargantuan, jagged wings flapped deafeningly, drowning out all other sounds.

With sharp, piercing black eyes, the flying creatures stared down menacingly at the human intruders. Frozen in terror, the group was assaulted by the birds' vile and unnatural display of hate. No one dared to move but their stillness enraged the birds even more. The huge, flying beasts squawked and cawed.

"Climb back down!" Dave screamed to his friends as he scrambled for a foothold. The ferocious birds swooped at them. In the climbers' haste to escape, first one and then another, tumbled head over heels down the craggy mountainside, banging and scraping themselves against the rocks.

The instant they were safely at the bottom of the slope, the sun shone brightly again and the sky was clear. Every one of the hundreds of vicious birds had vanished as quickly and mysteriously as they had appeared. It was like magic, a bizarre and evil kind of magic.

"I'll tell you, Kyle," Uncle Dave continued, "none of us has been the same since. Our cuts and bruises eventually healed but the terror of being threatened by hundreds of ghastly swarming birds has never been far from our minds since that day."

In a shivery whisper of a voice, Dave acknowledged that the adventurers were so tormented by the memory of their experience that, months later, they decided to investigate the types of birds they'd seen flying above them on that awful morning. They wanted very badly to prove to themselves that the ugly creatures were simply a species of hostile mountain-dwelling birds.

Sadly, the plan to ease their minds did not work. "An ornithologist, that's an expert on birds," Uncle Dave explained, "told us that such winged creatures did not exist, at least not now, not in this world. They haven't existed for thousands of years. He said these were *rocs*, prehistoric predators from the time of the dinosaurs. Like the dinosaurs, these flying creatures have been extinct for millions and millions of years. It seemed that those crazy old women weren't so crazy after all. Somehow they knew about those ancient, angry ghosts."

Kyle shrugged his shoulders to loosen the muscles that had tensed while he'd been listening to the story of his uncle's encounter with the supernatural. Dave took a deep breath and continued to talk but more to himself than to Kyle, it seemed.

"Some of the villagers say those birds are the ghosts of rocs while others believe that they're specters of people, thieves whose dishonest souls will forever haunt the places where their stolen treasures are hidden."

By the time Uncle Dave had finished telling of his encounter with the bizarre specters of doom, it was well after midnight and Kyle was so tired that he could barely climb the stairs to his bedroom but even so, it took a long time for him to fall asleep and when he finally did sleep it was not wonder that he was tormented by dreadful dreams of vicious birds.

The Jack O' Lantern Story

Have you ever wondered why we carve faces in pumpkins as part of our Halloween celebrations? The answer to that question is an interesting tale and, in part it's a ghost story, the story of a ghost doomed to walk the world's paths and trails forever.

Many hundreds of years ago, a man named Jack lived in an Irish village. Jack was not very popular with his neighbours because he was stingy. He would take whatever he could without paying for it and never offered anything to those in need. As the years went by and Jack got older, he became even more stingy and selfish. The tight-fisted man wouldn't share anything with anyone but would always take what was offered to him.

This unpopular fellow also liked to visit the local pub and sip an ice-cold beverage or two. When the other customers saw Stingy Jack coming, they usually scurried for home because he would pester them until they agreed to pay for his drinks.

On top of being miserly, Jack was also not very smart and, as a result, one day he invited the devil himself, Satan, to go to the pub with him. Satan accepted the invitation and the two enjoyed a drink together.

As usual, when it came time to pay for the drinks, Stingy Jack looked around for someone to help him out. This time, the place was empty. Everyone else had already gone home.

Jack suggested that Satan turn himself into money. "I'll pay for the drinks that way, my friend," the cheapskate explained. Oddly, the devil agreed.

Not only was Jack stingy and not very bright, but he was also a liar. As soon as Satan turned himself into money, Jack stuffed the coins into his pocket and sneaked away from the pub without paying.

Usually it's tough to feel sorry for Satan, but the poor devil was stuck in Stingy Jack's deep, dark pockets among chunks of lint the size of his big toes. It was pretty disgusting. Worse, Satan needed to get free in order to change himself back into his usual devilish shape.

"Let me out! Let me out!" Satan screamed from his pocket prison.

By this time, Stingy Jack was beginning to realize that he had made a big mistake. He was not dealing with just an ordinary person. Satan possessed frightening and dangerous powers. Besides, the devilish caterwauling coming from his pocket was annoying Jack.

"I'll release you as long as you promise not to steal my soul," Stingy Jack told Satan, who agreed to the bargain right away. Of course anyone with even a little bit of sense would not trust the devil's word, especially when that same devil was angry after being jostled around in a miserable man's pocket for the better part of a day.

But it was Jack's lucky day. As soon as he scooped the coins from his pocket and set them on the ground, the devil reappeared before him. The two looked at each other and ran in opposite directions.

Over the years, Stingy Jack didn't change very much. Eventually, he grew very old and died. Amazingly, the devil kept his word. He didn't send the cheating cheapskate straight to his eternal punishment but not all beings were that generous to the man's spirit. When Jack reached the Pearly Gates, he was turned away. "We don't want the likes of you up here, Stingy Jack," heaven's gatekeeper told him.

What was a wretched soul to do? He wasn't wanted anywhere, neither in heaven nor in hell. It seemed that the man who had been so mean to others in life was doomed to be miserable in his eternal afterlife. Stingy Jack had nowhere to go but back to earth. There his soul would stay, forever, wandering the earth's paths aimlessly, never resting.

Because he couldn't stop wandering even to sleep at nights, Jack took a glowing lump of coal that he had found by the roadside and placed it in a hollowed-out turnip. That way at least he would have a bit of light to guide his way during the dark of night.

Before long, the people of the countryside began to notice Jack and his strange lantern. Eventually, someone recognized him. "Why, that's the specter of Stingy Jack," the person announced. Some folks may even have smiled when they realized that Jack's spirit would never rest. Most people though, were just plain frightened. After all, Jack was a miserable enough fellow in life. Surely in death his mood would be even worse. Children shivered in their beds at the thought of Stingy Jack's ghost at their window late at night.

Perhaps out of respect for the dead, or perhaps not to risk angering the ghost any further, people stopped calling their former neighbour "Stingy Jack." More and more often, as the phantom wandered along the Irish country roads, villagers would call out to one another "Jack of the Lantern walks again tonight."

Even so, seeing the supernatural image wandering the roadways of his afterlife sent chills down the spines of all the children and many adults.

In the end though, Jack of the Lantern, gave the villagers an idea of how to keep his gruesome ghost away from their houses. First on one doorstep, then on a second and soon on all the doorsteps in town, large turnips, much like the one Jack carried, appeared when night fell.

Just as Jack had done, the townsfolk hollowed out the vegetable but before placing a burning lump of coal inside, they took one extra step. They carved faces into their turnips—ugly and scary faces that they hoped would frighten away evil spirits, including Jack's

The years went by. Jack's ghostly energy must have weakened because he was no longer seen walking through the Irish towns. Eventually the villagers stopped putting vegetables with glowing, menacing faces on their doorsteps. Except, that is, on one very special and very scary night of the year.

You see, according to ancient Celtic folklore, summer ends at sundown on October 31 and winter begins at sun-up on November 1. The hours between sundown and sun-up on that day belong to neither summer nor winter. Those hours are not really of this natural world and during that time there is no barrier between this life and the afterlife so spirits can roam among the living. Unless they protected their homes from all of those spirits, not just Jack of the Lantern's spirit, the people feared they would encounter beings from beyond this world. And so, to be safe from the supernatural, on that one night of every year, they kept to their old tradition.

Centuries later, when many of the people from that Irish village and others, sailed across the Atlantic Ocean to settle in North America, they brought their traditions, including the Jack-o'-lantern, with them.

Not long after the newcomers reached the New World, they learned about the many bounties in their chosen homeland, including a wonderful vegetable called a pumpkin. Not only was this pretty orange vegetable tasty and healthy, it made a much more effective Jack-o'-lantern than a turnip did.

And so, thanks to a ghost who was doomed to wander the world's highways and byways, pumpkins and Halloween are linked together forever.

Forever Haunted

For those of us who live in North America, India seems a world away. That country bustles with crowds of exotically dressed people, brilliant colors, lush vegetation and unfamiliar sounds and smells. Tourists in India have so much to see and hear and taste and smell and touch that it can become too much to deal with and people have been known to get horribly confused and frightened.

During World War II, American soldiers were often stationed in India at a military camp near the city of Calcutta. Because this area was so different than any place most of them had ever been before, the soldiers were often very uneasy in their temporary home. Richard was one such soldier. Many years after the war was over and he was safely back home in the United States, Richard still remembered exactly how terror-stricken he had been during his first-ever guard duty there.

Even the trek to get to the temporary military quarters had been difficult. The men were surrounded by strange and unfriendly noises as they hacked through thick, dark, damp overgrown vines and past a pile of tumbled-down rocks and stones that, years ago, had been a beautiful temple.

Once the soldiers arrived at the camp, two men were chosen to keep watch for the night while the others slept. Richard was one of those ordered to stand guard. As he was part of a unit that paired soldiers with trained dogs, the young man would at least have his dog to keep him company during the overnight watch. On the other side of the camp, another soldier and his dog would be doing the same.

As Richard patrolled, he was disgusted to discover flying insects, crawling bugs, quirky lizards and slithering snakes. He might have wondered how much worse the night could be. If so, he was about to find out in a particularly eerie, supernatural way, when the noises and movements that had been making him feel so uncomfortable suddenly stopped. Complete silence and stillness encircled him. Seconds later, the dog by his side and the other dogs in their pens began to shift about, restlessly squirming and whimpering as though they were newborn pups instead of the specially chosen and highly trained adult dogs that they were.

Richard reached down to give his own dog a reassuring pat but yanked his arm back again quickly when he felt the hair on the back of the animal's neck standing straight up and he heard a vicious growl build in the dog's throat. Still having no idea what was happening or what he should do to save himself or his fellow soldiers, Richard slowly turned around. He thought he'd heard a sound far off in the distance. He listened as the noise grew louder and louder until he finally recognized it. It was the thundering of horses' hooves galloping toward the camp at top speed. A herd of steeds was charging toward him from the direction of the old crumbled temple they had passed on their route into the base.

Terrified, Richard drew his gun. But what could he shoot at? Nothing was visible in the inky black that surrounded him but still the terrible sounds pounded louder and louder against his eardrums. Dozens of stampeding horses were charging directly at him. The hooves of the galloping herd made the ground beneath his feet vibrate. With that new sensation, Richard gave up trying to be strong. There was no way, on his own, that he was going to be able to protect the others. He would have no alternative but to sound the alarm.

No doubt he would have done so, if he'd had time but Richard had no sooner reached that decision than his dog reared up and lunged against its leash with such force that it sent Richard flying face first, flat on the ground. As the man lay there, paralyzed with fear, he felt a great rush of cool, damp wind whirl past him. That night at midnight in the Indian jungle near Calcutta, Richard listened, terror stricken, as dozens of horses headed directly toward him as he lay in the dirt.

Just as the young man was sure he was going to faint from fear, the sounds began to recede into the distance on the other side of the camp until the thundering hooves were mere whispers once again. Then, just as suddenly as the noises had begun, they stopped. Richard had not seen a thing, not even one horse, nor had he been hurt, let alone killed.

The immediate danger had apparently passed, but Richard's fright hadn't. It took him days afterward to calm down. His friends asked over and over what it was that was bothering him, but the man would not say a word about the phantom horses. Such an admission would invite dreadful teasing at the very least.

Less than a week after his experience with the paranormal, Richard heard some interesting local history. It seems that the tumble-down temple near the base camp was said to be an evil place. Those who lived in the area would not go near the ruins. They had seen and heard hundreds of the ghosts that haunted it, including the spirits of charging horses and their memories of those encounters stayed with them for the rest of their lives.

Richard knew then that, on a dark night during his World War II guard duty in India, he had become, and would remain, one of those haunted people.

Ghosts in Ghost Towns

The town of Barkerville in northern British Columbia, Canada is a ghost town that's full of ghosts! The Royal Theatre on Main Street is particularly haunted.

People hear the sounds of footsteps walking across the stage even when no one is near the stage. A ghostly dancer once joined a group of performers on stage but vanished before curtain call. Another ghost that has been seen over the years is an apparition described as being dressed in formal evening-wear and sporting a distinctive moustache.

And then there's the supernatural phantom music. Performers relaxing during a rehearsal break listened to lovely music echoing throughout the theater despite the fact the speaker system in the building was turned off. Then, a few minutes later, they heard a woman singing. The group searched the entire building but never found a rational explanation for the ghostly music so they just accepted the serenade as calmly as they could, knowing that they were in a haunted building.

Apparently the show must go on, even beyond the curtain of time.

The Haunted Bird Cage

Tombstone, Arizona is another ghost town with a haunted theater. It's really no wonder this old place is haunted because, back in the day, some of the greatest characters in the Wild West visited The Bird Cage. Jesse James, Wild Bill Hickok, Wyatt Earp, Doc Holliday and Bat Masterson all spent time in the theater.

Like the Royal Theatre in Barkerville, phantom sounds are heard in the building. The ghostly sounds of outlaws' card games still echo throughout the Bird Cage and the ghosts of long-dead performers still appear on the stage.

One of the most commonly seen ghosts is dressed in black pinstriped pants and walks from stage right to stage left. Then he stops to look at the clipboard he's carrying before he vanishes to the great beyond. People who work in the theater these days are sure he's the spirit of a stagehand who once worked at the Bird Cage.

Another resident spirit is a white-haired man wearing a white shirt. He's especially interesting because he's always seen at the theater's front door. Then he steps outside the building onto the sidewalk and looks around before going back inside and disappearing. This often occurs even when the theater doors are locked closed.

Still another ghost is recognized as being the current theater owner's grandfather.

While many spirits don't seem aware of today's world, one phantom at the Bird Cage interacts with the living! An employee who was locking the building one night approached the apparition and asked, "Can I help you?" The ghost answered, "I'm looking for my wife."

The employee suggested that the wraith walk downstairs with her and he did. There were a few people clustered at the bottom of the stairs including an older woman. The employee held out her hand toward the lady and asked, "Ma'am, is this your husband?" The woman gave a puzzled look. When the employee turned back toward the man she saw the reason for the woman's quizzical look. The image had disappeared as mysteriously as it had appeared.

Phantom smells, such as whisky and cigar smoke from long ago, still waft through the theater even though there's no smoking or drinking allowed in the building these days.

The owners and staff at this historic theater know that they're never alone in the building but that doesn't bother them. As a matter of fact, they treat their ghostly colleagues with dignity and respect. It seems the Bird Cage Theater in Tombstone, Arizona is a fine place to live out your afterlife.

Roman Horses

Matt's encounter with ghosts occurred many years ago, but it was such a startling experience that he still remembers it well.

Matt was visiting his grandparents in England that summer and he and his grandfather were driving along a narrow country road when they noticed that a big clump of bushes off to the side of the road was moving. Matt's grandfather slowed the car a bit and they both stared. At first they couldn't see anything beyond this odd movement. Then, just a few feet ahead, a horse appeared on the road. Matt's grandfather slammed his foot on the brake pedal but the car didn't stop right away. The tires skidded along the gravel surface while another horse and then another and another, walked calmly out onto the road in front of the car. They could see the huge animals clearly.

All Matt and his grandfather could do was stare in horror and hold their breath, hoping the car would stop in time. Then, the worst happened. As Grandpa's car skidded,

146

they hit the last horse in the procession. Matt's grandfather jumped out of the car with Matt not far behind. The two expected to find the car badly dented and a horse lying on the road.

But there was nothing on the road and the car didn't even have a scratch on it. Matt and his grandfather looked around in complete bewilderment. There were no signs that any horse had been anywhere near the area. There weren't even any hoof marks in the dirt.

They shook their heads, their minds and hearts racing. They drove home in silence, each one thinking his own thoughts about what had just happened. By the time they arrived back at the house, Matt had replayed the bizarre incident over and over in his mind. He'd come to the conclusion that those horses looked different than any other horses he'd ever seen and he'd certainly never seen saddles like those before.

Matt expected that his grandfather would want to talk about their experience but the older man didn't say a word. It was as though the encounter had never occurred. This was a bit disappointing because by evening Matt's curiosity had ramped into high gear.

The next day he hopped on his bike and rode into town. He knew there was a library in a little building just off the main street and that's where he went. He took down book after book about horses to see if he could find even one picture of a horse that looked like the ones he and his grandfather had nearly hit.

Finally he found a drawing of a saddled horse from the Roman era when Caesar had invaded the British Isles—in the year 55 BC.

Those must've been Roman horses we saw, the ghosts of steeds that trod through the forests of the English countryside thousands of years ago, Matt thought. *Those horses were definitely there. We both saw them but they were not really on this earthly plane with us.*

Those horses had cantered through the veil of time. The only question that remained was whether the Roman horses had come to Matt and his grandfather's time or whether Matt and his grandfather had, for just a few moments, somehow found their way back to the exact moment in history when those horses had crossed that particular stretch of country road.

Haunted Hooves

The grand old estate of Thorpe Hall in Lincolnshire, England is home to the sound of horses' hooves stepping along a gravel path in front of that building. What makes these sounds especially spooky is that there hasn't been a gravel path for many centuries and when the noises are heard there aren't any horses in sight. Despite this, the clip-clopping of the hooves, followed by crunching gravel, as if from wagon wheels can often be clearly heard.

Witnesses say the sounds come closer and closer until they seem to be right in front of the haunted building. Then, just as mysteriously and invisibly as they started, the noises fade off into the distance. People who've heard these inexplicable sounds are sure that a horse-drawn coach has just driven past. The trouble is, the witnesses haven't seen a thing. These phantom sounds are apparently echoes of a time long ago.

Never Forgotten

Near Moravian Falls, North Carolina, three girls were walking down a country road near the farm where they lived with their parents. Suddenly they heard the distinctive sounds of horses' hooves followed by the rattle of wagon wheels coming up behind them. They'd grown up around horses and wagons so they knew to move over to the side of the road and let the team pass but when they looked along the road they couldn't see anything at all.

Despite this, the sounds grew louder. They listened in fear as the hoof beats came closer and closer until they passed beside the girls and then slowly faded off into the distance. Terrified, the trio ran for home and told their parents what had happened but the adults were as confused as the children were.

Those three youngsters are adults themselves now but they've never forgotten their experience that day on the country road. They still talk of the day they heard, but didn't see, a horse and wagon. Of course, by now they understand that the experience was a paranormal encounter.

Bogus Bus to Blame

There are an amazing number of tales about phantom buses, perhaps because buses (both phantom and real) generally travel over and over again along busy routes that lots of people use. There's even been a report of a police officer chasing a spectral bus through a red light. It's difficult to imagine whether the officer was relieved or upset to learn that he or she had been trying to ticket a driver who had been dead for many years.

One of the best-documented cases of a phantom bus causing a real collision was reported in London, England, in 1934 when a young man was driving his car through an intersection. He noticed a bus coming toward him so fast that he was positive they were going to collide. The young driver twisted the steering wheel as hard as he could which sent his car straight into the path of a truck. The truck and the car slammed into each other, scattering broken bits of metal and glass all around. Fortunately, no one was seriously injured.

At the exact moment that the two vehicles hit, people nearby reported that they had watched a bus travel straight through the accident scene. Afterwards, many of those people commented that the bus seemed to glide through the smashed cars as though it wasn't solid.

Investigators later discovered that a phantom bus was often seen crossing the street at that very spot!

WRAITH ON THE ROAD

Just south of Carmel-by-the-Sea along California's coast there is a roadway that passes a beautiful castle-like building which, in turn, overlooks a white sandy beach. The building may look like a castle but in reality it is an old monastery. Roughly halfway between the beach and the monastery is a stretch of road that looks perfectly normal but is closer to being paranormal because motorists often have to suddenly steer around "a long-ago lady," who seems to be very unconcerned about the traffic around her. No one knows who the ghost was when she was alive but her image has been seen since that stretch of highway opened in 1937.

Children's Laughter

Wilma lived alone in an apartment in New York City. One morning she was startled awake by the sound of children crying in the hallway outside her door. She got up from bed and peered out into the hall. The corridor was empty and yet she could still hear their cries.

Wilma listened carefully. Suddenly she knew that these were echoes of her sister Thelma's children. But they lived in Chicago! Concerned, Wilma phoned her sister right away.

"I knew you would call," Thelma told her. "I willed the children's cries to you because I'm so sick that I can't look after them. Can you come and help me please?"

That evening Wilma boarded a plane and flew to be with her sister. By the end of the week Thelma was much better and able to manage on her own but neither sister ever understood what power had caused the cries from children in Chicago to be heard in New York City.

WALTER THE MULE

As far back as 13-year-old Jamal could remember, his neighbour, Miss Wilson had been old. The woman had a wrinkly face and scraggly grayish hair. She was all stooped over and walked so slowly.

Jamal knew that Miss Wilson had lived all her life in their small, quiet village. He was pretty sure that no one ever went to visit Miss Wilson. Jamal knew that when he collected the money from his paper route customers, the old woman was the only one who didn't speak to him. She just handed him some money and then closed the wooden door to her run-down cottage.

Everyone in the village pretty much left their strange old neighbour alone. Perhaps they felt uncomfortable with her odd ways and that was a perfectly understandable reaction, because the old lady seemed to spend every hour of every day with her only friend, Walter the mule.

Jamal thought a dog would've been a more sensible choice for a pet because Walter was a stodgy old mule that smelled really, really bad. He smelled so bad that even people blocks away would catch the unpleasant odour.

Miss Wilson and Walter both looked pretty odd too. The old lady always wore big, heavy, dirty work boots and a greasy apron over a faded print dress. She wore a battered hat that might have been a fancy-dress Easter hat back in the day. Walter, believe it or not, also wore a hat, a lacy bonnet, like the ones Jamal had seen on babies in old family photos. A bonnet on a mule is a weird enough sight but, somehow, because he was a boy mule wearing a girl's hat, he looked even stranger.

Jamal had never, not even once, seen Miss Wilson outside without her smelly, funny-looking mule right beside her, nor had he ever seen the old woman with any other human being. Odder still, Miss Wilson talked to Walter almost constantly. Jamal had heard her say things like, "Well, it looks like we're going to get some rain, Walter. What do you think?" and "Oh, what's the matter with these peonies, Walter? Why aren't their petals as soft as the ones from last year?"

But the clincher was that when Miss Wilson spoke to Walter, the mule looked back at her. It seemed to Jamal as though the funny-looking, stinky mule understood every word she said.

Sadly, one summer's day, Miss Wilson's beloved Walter died. Poor Miss Wilson, now she was completely alone. Her only friend in the world was gone.

Because Jamal delivered the newspaper to Miss Wilson's house every day, he could see that she was horribly lonely after Walter's death. One evening, he talked to his mom and she and several other neighbours got together and decided that what Miss Wilson needed was another mule to keep her company. The very next day, Jamal's mom and some of the other villagers approached the woman's cottage.

"We would like to buy you a new mule," they told Miss Wilson when she answered their knocks at her door.

After only a few moments thought, the lonely old woman told her neighbours, "No. Thank you for your offer, but no other animal could ever replace my Walter." With that, Miss Wilson quickly and firmly closed her cottage door.

A few months later, in the damp chill of a late autumn morning, Jamal was delivering newspapers when he came across something that stopped him dead in his tracks.

What's that? Jamal wondered when he saw what looked like a heap of clothing in Miss Wilson's yard. *Is she getting forgetful? It looks as though she's left her sweater outside overnight. I'd better take it to her door.* He opened the gate to the old woman's backyard but the sight before him startled Jamal like he'd never been startled before. He just stood there, bewildered. It looked (and smelled!) as if Miss Wilson's old mule, Walter, his bonnet slightly askew, was lying beside her sweater. Jamal knew that what he was seeing and smelling couldn't possibly be real. That animal had died months ago. Worse, closer inspection revealed that it was not just Walter and Miss Wilson's sweater that were in front of him and on the ground, but also Miss Wilson herself, collapsed in a heap.

What should I do? Jamal wondered. *I don't want to go near that spooky mule and I certainly don't want to touch Miss Wilson. How can they both still smell this horrible when I know that the mule is dead?* Suddenly, Jamal thought of something even more horrible. *What if she's alive now and then she dies while I waste time deciding what to do?*

With a big, deep breath, the boy mustered all the courage he could. He set down his pile of newspapers and moved closer to Miss Wilson's almost lifeless body. He crouched down and put his hand on her shoulder. "Miss Wilson, what's wrong?" Jamal asked. He was jiggling the woman's arm and hoping desperately that she would open her eyes.

Jamal's fright level skyrocketed when he noticed that Walter's smelly image had moved and was now standing right beside him. For a while, the phantom animal looked straight into Jamal's eyes, with his bonnet hanging down over one ear.

Then Walter's ghost slowly trotted off toward the road.

As the mule's apparition reached the curb, it stopped, turned its head back toward Jamal and looked him straight in the eye. For a moment, the newspaper boy and the ghost mule stared at one another. Then the animal's apparition vanished from sight. That's when the boy knew for certain that he had seen a ghost.

By the time Jamal looked back down at the old woman still lying on the ground, she was opening her eyes. *She's alive!* He helped Miss Wilson get to her feet and then, very slowly, he led the weakened woman into her house. As soon as she was safely inside, Jamal raced to fetch the town's doctor, who quickly followed the boy back to Miss Wilson's side.

After running some medical tests, the doctor suggested that she had simply not been taking care of herself properly since Walter had died. He was sure that Miss Wilson would recuperate fully within a couple of weeks if she rested. And, as it turned out, he was quite correct. Ten days later, Miss Wilson was feeling well enough to work in her garden and to go for walks.

But now she had a friend because Jamal was often at her side. She told him how frightened she'd been when she thought she was going to die alone in her garden. She also explained how comforted she'd been when she'd felt Walter beside her. She said it had been Walter who had kept her warm until Jamal arrived.

Miss Wilson lived to be very, very old. And, though he always swore that he could smell that terrible stink of Walter around her, Jamal continued to help her so, in a way, the mule's ghost even brought her the friend she so badly needed.

As for Jamal, not only did he enjoy his friendship with the town's oddest resident, but also, when he and his friends gathered around a campfire, he was the only one who could tell a true ghost story!

No Grass on the Grave

Many years ago, a man in Wales was sentenced to death for a crime he claimed he hadn't committed. With his last breath he proclaimed, "I am innocent and no grass will grow over my grave for a generation to prove it."

His body was buried at the edge of the local churchyard. Even though no one really believed the man's dying threat, they were extra careful as they replaced the sod over his grave. In a matter of days, however, the groundskeepers noticed that the grass had died and the bare spot was in the shape of a coffin. They quickly replaced the sod but once again the grass died off—in that same recognizable shape.

This time the workers put fresh soil down over the grave and then added special grass seed, but all to no avail. It seemed as though the dead man had made good his threat. It also seemed as though they had hanged an innocent man.

By then everyone was afraid to go near that part of the churchyard. Finally, after thirty years, grass began to grow but only as an outline of a coffin and as far as anyone knows that's how it remains to this day.

Bugsy's Bogey

For a while, way back in the 1940s, a woman named Virginia lived in a grand home in the Beverly Hills area of Los Angeles. The mansion's stately white columns stretched from the beautifully manicured lawns up to the red-slate roof. Every detail of the house was luxurious. Even the windows were huge and grandly rounded at the top. Interestingly it was one of those windows that caused the house to become haunted.

Back in those days, criminals often formed mobs. One of the worst of these mobsters was a man nicknamed "Bugsy." Bugsy was as handsome as a movie star and a lot of people thought he was pretty smart. But his actions sometimes told a different story. The last and dumbest of his crimes was to steal money from other criminals! After that, it wasn't just the police who were after Bugsy, his fellow criminals were out to get him too.

Bugsy was visiting Virginia in that beautiful mansion with the grand windows when the angry bad guys found him. It was all over in about a minute. A car full of the robbers that Bugsy had robbed, pulled up in front of Virginia's house just as Bugsy was walking through the living room. The mobsters ran onto the lawn and fired their machine guns at the man in the window. Seconds later, they were gone and Bugsy was dead.

It would be difficult to imagine a more sudden or brutal death. Some people said the spray of bullets was so powerful that one of Bugsy's eyes was knocked right out of his head and clear across the room! Others simply said that justice had been done.

Virginia moved away from Beverly Hills that very day. Someone else would have to look after the gruesome job of cleaning Bugsy's blood off the walls and ceiling and floors and maybe even looking around for his eye. Virginia wasn't going to stay around to see who got stuck with the job. Bugsy himself, however, apparently stayed behind. Well, his spirit did at least.

At first, no one wanted to live in the house where the murder had taken place. Psychics who visited the vacant house all came away saying that Bugsy's ghost was definitely there. They said that his death had been so sudden that his spirit was frozen where the hail of bullets had ended his life.

After a few months, most people forgot about the grisly murder and the fact that the splendid mansion was haunted. Soon a family with three teenage boys moved into the house. The mother of the family, Martha, always felt especially fond of her family's new home. When people asked her why she liked the house so well, Martha usually smiled and said that she felt protected there.

One night, that protected feeling left her for a moment. Martha had been sleeping soundly when she was startled awake by noises coming from the living room. At first she was frightened by the sounds but then she decided that one of her sons was up in the middle of the night.

The woman rose from her bed and headed toward the stairs to tell the boys to be quiet and go back to bed. As she was about to take the first step down the stairs, Martha felt someone's breath on her ear. She knew she was alone, but she felt a presence and then clearly heard a man's whispery voice tell her, "Don't go downstairs. There are robbers in your house."

Quietly, she turned around and crept back into her bedroom, got into bed and pulled the covers up over her head until the noises downstairs stopped. Only then did she pick up the phone and call the police who got there in time to arrest the burglars.

Everyone else in the family felt upset about the robbery. Martha just felt relieved that her life had been saved by her very own special security system—the ghost of a gangster. Maybe because bad guys had killed Bugsy himself, his ghost was determined to save other people from criminals.

The Phantom House

Cheryl knew she shouldn't have stayed at Tracy's Christmas party for so long, but she'd been having such fun with her friends that the hours had just flown past. By the time she said good-bye, brushed the snow off her car and began the drive back to the city, it was well after midnight.

She had only driven a few miles when the wind picked up, whipping the falling snow into a fierce blizzard. Cheryl knew she shouldn't be driving in this storm; the road conditions were definitely not safe. Each minute seemed to take forever as she slowly drove on, every muscle in her body tense. Before long she was choking back terrified sobs.

"I could die out here!" she screamed inside her head. "Someone help me, please! Someone! Anyone! I'm only 18! Don't let me die! Help!"

Then, was she imagining it or had the wind died down a bit? Could she see a bit farther ahead now? Glancing to her right, Cheryl thought she saw a long low stone fence. Moments later, her car's headlights shone on a huge, open gate attached to stone pillars. *That must mean a house is nearby,* she reasoned.

As Cheryl drove through the gate, the snow and wind died down even more. She hadn't driven far when she was able to make out the faint outline of a two-storey house just ahead. Relief washed over her. She was sure that inside that house she would find someone to help her.

Driving the car close to the house, Cheryl could see lights on in the upstairs window of the big old place. *Thank goodness,* she thought. *Whoever lives here is home. They're probably getting ready for bed.*

Cheryl jumped from her car and went up the porch steps to the front door. Her heart thumping, she knocked on the door, but her heavy mitts muffled the sound. There was no knocker on the door and no doorbell. Pulling off her mitts and sobbing with frustration, she banged on the door as hard as she could, but there was no answer.

A scream built in her throat. She was so close to safety and yet she was still in great danger. Morning was a long time away and she badly needed shelter. She could freeze to death out there! Drawing in a deep breath she firmly twisted the doorknob to the right. Slowly, the door opened. She was saved!

"Hello?" Cheryl called out as she stepped into the warmth of the house and closed the door behind her. When no one responded to her call, Cheryl began to make her way up the staircase directly in front of her.

The upstairs lights were on, she reasoned. *I guess no one could hear me because they're up there. Sure hope I don't scare anyone.*

Calling out "Hello! Hello!" the girl made her way up the darkened staircase. As her foot hit the top step she froze. Whoever had the lights on must be able to hear her now. *What if some madman's hiding and waiting for me?* she wondered in a panic.

Gathering her last bit of courage, Cheryl tiptoed toward the room where the light was shining brightly. "Hello! Hello! Hello!" she called but no one answered.

As she went into the room, she told herself that the family who lived in the house must have gone out and left the lights on. The bedroom looked so inviting. A big, pale blue easy chair was over by the window and there was a four-poster bed made up with the prettiest bedclothes Cheryl had ever seen. The pink comforter looked so soft and inviting that she couldn't help but run her hand over it. As she did, the terror she'd just been through slipped from her mind. She was so tired that she couldn't keep her eyes open even a second longer. Shrugging off her coat and kicking off her boots, she climbed between the covers of the bed and instantly fell asleep.

Hours later, sunbeams pouring through the window of the strange room awakened the young woman. For an instant, she couldn't remember where she was or why she was there. Frightened at first, Cheryl sat up. As she did, memories of the terrifying drive came flooding back. Easing herself from the bed, she realized that she was still alone and that the big old house might well have saved her life that cruel winter night. Better still, she felt calm and well rested. She'd had one of the best sleeps of her entire life.

If I leave right now, no one will even know I've been here, the girl thought. She quickly made the bed, pulled on her boots, grabbed her coat and scampered down the stairs. Outside, bright sunlight glinted on the newly fallen snow. The world looked like a winter wonderland. With a smile of relief, Cheryl settled herself into her car and backed down the driveway toward the gate and onto the road.

The snow plow must've been along through the night, she noted with thanks.

Soon Cheryl was back in her own apartment. *What an adventure,* she thought as she made herself a cup of hot chocolate and called Tracy to let her know she was safely home.

Tracy was very glad to hear from her friend. As Cheryl was explaining all the events of the night before; the terrible driving conditions and the welcoming house with the wonderful bed; Tracy became silent. When she finally found her voice, it was weak with confusion and concern.

"You couldn't have stayed at that house, Cheryl. I know exactly the place you mean, the gate between the stone pillars. I drove past there the other day. There is no house anymore. There's just a pile of ashes. That place burned to the ground last month."

Then it was Cheryl who couldn't find her voice.

Quietly Tracy spoke again. "I have to come into the city on Saturday anyway. I'll take some pictures of where the house used to be. There's nothing left of it. It's just a pile of burned-out timber and ashes."

Cheryl was bewildered almost beyond speech. She croaked out a few words to Tracy and then the two friends said good-bye.

By sundown on Saturday, Cheryl had seen Tracy's pictures on the computer screen. She recognized the stone fence and even the driveway leading to the house but the house that was not there. As she stared at her screen she finally realized that, on that dark and stormy night, she had been saved by a paranormal encounter. Cheryl had spent the night in a phantom house!

Barbara Smith has written so many books of true ghost stories that she sometimes forgets exactly how many! She never forgets though that kids are her favourite readers. You can find Barbara on Facebook or check out some of her other collections—*Ghost Stories of California, Ghost Stories of the Rocky Mountains, Haunted Theaters* and at least thirty more titles.

Made in United States
North Haven, CT
26 September 2022

24570187R00096